The Mum Job
Asha Rebel-Lammersen

Contents

"There's a bit of magic in everything, and some loss to even things out."
- *Lou Reed, 'Magic And Loss'*

"There is a sacredness in tears. They are not the mark of weakness, but of power. They speak more eloquently than ten thousand tongues. They are the messengers of overwhelming grief, of deep contrition, and of unspeakable love."
- *Washington Irving*

To Hilde; your bravery, resilience, and endurance serve as a shining example to all of us.

Chapter One

I've seen my fair share of waiting rooms, but this one takes boredom to a whole new level. White walls, no posters or colourful paintings, no fluffy chairs, no magazines to pass time, and not even a reception desk to register at when you walk in. I don't understand why I'm here in the first place, or how long I've been here. Time is a funny concept, though. People always talk about how time flies when they're having fun. I didn't exactly enjoy myself these past three years, yet time flew by anyway. During hospital visits, Dad would repeatedly tell me he wished he could turn back time, if only for a couple of years. Mum, on the other hand, kept telling everyone that if she had a magic wand, she'd stop time. Neither of my parents got what they wished for. Time moved on as usual. The hospital visits became more frequent and my treatment more demanding. Until that moment where time came to a standstill, at least for me, that is. I don't remember much of those last few days. I was asleep most of the time. However, I can recall what the room looked like. It wasn't as dreadful as the one I'm in now. On the contrary, it had soft yellow walls decorated with a flowery pattern. There was this huge window facing south, letting in so much light I seriously considered using sun cream when I first moved in. My bed was comfy, but had all these machines and electronic equipment stationed next to it, which was a bit of a buzz kill to be honest. To give the room a positive vibe, my parents and friends joined forces by pimping the space to a degree, that it looked as if Build a Bear had invaded a flower shop. There were cuddly toys everywhere, neatly placed between a dozen or so colourful arrangements in clear vases. Two helium gas 'get well soon' balloons were attached to the railing of my bed, happily floating in the air. Needless to say I appreciated the sentiment, although the 'get well soon' wishes didn't exactly resonate with the reality of my situation. I wasn't going to get well soon. In fact, I wasn't going to get well ever again.

So here I am, biding my time in what I can only describe as the most miserable place to start your afterlife. Unless I'm not destined to start one at all. What if I got sent to hell, and this is where I'll be for the rest of eternity? Doesn't make any sense though. What could a twenty-one-year-old college student have possibly done to be dumped in such a desolate place? 'Come on Calum, think'. I rack my brain for any serious transgressions, but looking back on my short-lived life, I can't really come up with anything. Of course, I haven't always been a saint, but I can't imagine being shipped off to this barren room for nicking sweets, ditching class, or that one time I 'borrowed' my mum's Vespa. I went over to my friend's place, had a few drinks and ended up driving it into a ditch on the way back. I was sixteen at the time, and rather lucky to have got away with just a few bumps and scratches. My mum called it my 'get out of jail free card', cause if I would ever pull something like that again she'd drag my bum to the nearest police station herself. So I decided to get my act together, and focus on getting into college. There was this sports management course I had my eyes set on for years. Can't have a bad rep or a criminal record when you want to become a successful athletic trainer. Not to mention the fact that I had soccer practise three times a week, a match every weekend, and I'd throw in some gym sessions in between. Hangovers and daily exercise do not go well together. In my senior year, I decided to find another way to blow off steam. I downloaded this app on my phone and occasionally hooked up with other dudes in my area. I liked to keep things casual, cause nurturing a relationship takes time and effort. I wanted to invest my time in achieving goals of my own, without having to alter them, or slow them down for anyone else's sake. In due course, I would find someone to settle down with, but not before I made my own way in life. Unfortunately, life took a different turn, and I achieved none of the objectives I hoped for.

"Uhm Calum Jones?"

I am so lost in my own thoughts, I never heard anyone coming in. I turn around to see a woman in a crisp three piece suit, holding a clipboard, and a pen.

"You're Calum Jones right?"

"Yes, I am."

"I am Olga Jensen-Scott but, but please call me Olga."

"Right, well I am Calum. Oh wait, you already seem to know that. Uhm, I'm feeling a bit overwhelmed. Where am I?"

"That's perfectly understandable Calum, you're in the waiting room."

"Waiting room? I thought I'd died."

"You did. That's why you're in the waiting room."

"Sorry, but that doesn't really clarify anything. If I died, why am I in a waiting room?"

"Good question Calum. That's where everyone goes who crosses over before we decide what happens next."

"Oh good, cause for a moment I thought I ended up in hell."

"Why would you think that?"

"Have you looked around? This is a pretty uninspiring place. There is literally nothing here."

"I see what you mean. Thing is, not everyone has an easy cross over. Some are actually quite violent and traumatic. We keep this room as trigger free as we possibly can, as not to inflict any more pain or discomfort."

"Oh, I understand. Have I been here for long?"

"Time works a bit different up here than down below. It's not a linear thing with a beginning and an end. Hope you haven't worried too much, though."

"A bit. I was trying to figure out if I had done anything bad to end up in an empty waiting room all by myself."

"You have nothing to worry about. Apart from one DUI offense, you're actually a pretty decent guy."

"Thank you. Just to make sure you've got your intel right, I'm gay."

"So?"

"Well, quite a few religions seem to take issue with that."

"Listen, I have never met our CEO. That's way above my paygrade. What I do know is that They created mankind in Their own image. That means that every gender and sexual orientation is justified. We had Pride up here way before you guys down there finally caught on. We kept throwing you hints though. Why do you think rainbows exist?"

"Wait what? So there are no religious grounds for homophobia?"

"Nope, it's something you down dwellers came up with all by yourselves."

"What about scripture and all those holy books that claim otherwise?"

"Look, I'm not a scholar, but I've been up here since way before Joseph got that girl Mary in the family way. He managed to pass it off as a divine miracle, although he certainly had a hand in it too. A couple of centuries before the little rug rat was born, society started to fall apart, and people turned against their families, friends and neighbours.

We thought that common ground would keep the peace and bring back some sort of stability. We started to inspire down dwellers to write down stories of hope, unconditional love, and selflessness. Somehow throughout time, quite a few of these tales became botched to an extend they didn't convey the message we initially wanted to put out there. Many down dwellers, mostly men, if I may be frank with you, started using our words of wisdom for personal gain, wealth and power. Our department of misinformation and fake news are working around the clock to turn things around, but that takes time. If things go south too fast, we'll just flood the place, and start all over again."

"Really?"

"Just kidding, you should have seen your face. Flooding didn't make a difference the first time, so we won't be going down that road again. Speaking of going, we should have been on our way like yesterday. Our job agency is expecting you."

Did she just say job agency? I don't have time to ask what that means, cause she's off, and it takes all I've got to keep up with her. She's so fast I wonder if her feet actually touch the ground. She seems to glide rather than walk. Olga guides me through hallways, taking turns every so often. I feel like I'm running around in a giant maze, where I have lost every sense of direction. Finally, we come to a stop in front of an oak wooden door. After a firm knock, we're told to come in. The room is way bigger than I thought it would be. It's an office space with people working in cubicles. At the back there's a big mahogany desk with a gentleman staring daggers at his computer.

"Gabe love, how are you today?"

"About to throw this damn thing out of the window, Olga. After last week's software update, my laptop keeps glitching. Can't get anything done here, and I'm far behind schedule as it is."

"Sorry to hear that. Have you reached out to IT yet?"

"I have, but ever since Mr Jobs decided to switch his focus to bitcoin, our software updates are an absolute disaster."

"Well, I'm here with Calum Jones today. I've just picked him up from the waiting room."

Gabe looks up for the first time and stares at me for at least five uncomfortable seconds.

"Right, they keep getting younger, don't they? What a pity. So much potential wasted."

I scrape my throat and decide to take matters into my own hand.

"Uhm, Mr Gabe, I understand this is a job agency, but I have no idea what I'm doing here."

"Well, this one is a bit thick, isn't he, Olga? Haven't you brought him up to date yet?"

"Gabe, love, don't be rude. I think Calum has a lot going for him, and yes, I haven't entirely filled him in on this place yet. You're not the only one running behind schedule."

"Fine, my apologies Calum. Since Olga hasn't done her job, let me give you the lay of the land, so to speak. I assume you know that you've passed away. My condolences. I do hope your cross over wasn't too violent or traumatic."

As he's saying this, I have a feeling that's exactly what he was hoping for, but I keep quiet.

"Right now you're at the 'Afterlife Job Agency'. Welcome to your first day of eternity."

"Uhm, if I may ask, why do I have to get a job? As far as I know, I've just died. Can't I just get into, I don't know, heaven or something, and have a bit of a sit down?"

Gabe looks at me as if he's about to throw me out of the window along with his glitching computer screen, but he collects himself at the last moment. He takes a deep breath and swallows twice.

"What do you think happens when a person dies?" He asks me.

"Well, as I've learned in Sunday school, good people go to heaven or paradise, having an absolute blast doing whatever they like all day long. Bad people go to hell and burn for eternity."

"Darling, you couldn't be more wrong. Whenever someone over the age of eighteen passes, they end up in the waiting room. It is true that bad people don't get to come up here. They have to follow a re-education programme before they qualify for a position at the Afterlife Agency. That sort of thing can take centuries, though, and some don't make it here at all. But that's not my department, so let's not digress. Those who do make it here are assigned a position. That basically means helping out the living, or as we call them, down dwellers. When the job is done, you move on to your next assignment."

"For how long will I be doing this?"

"Eternity son. As long as there are down dwellers, there'll be jobs. They need all the help they can get making their miserable lives more tolerable. I don't know whose idea it was to give them free will, but it didn't do them any good."

"Do I get any time off, or vacation days?"

"A perk of being dead is that you don't need any sleep, rest, or time to recuperate. You don't need any food or drink to keep you going either. However, we don't want this place to be too bleak. So whenever you feel like you could use a break, you can recharge at our pub called the Cheeky Rooster. They have a lovely buffet, a great selection of wines, and every so often live performers."

"When I get assigned a job, what is it exactly that I have to do?"

"Every down dweller comes with a set of instructions. Don't worry about that. Since you're a newbie, you won't be getting any difficult cases. Just the average 'lonely gran needs to be looked after' or 'overworked nurse needs a break'."

"Right, but how can I help those people when I'm dead? I don't suppose resurrection is in the cards."

"Of course it isn't. Once you're dead, you're dead. Resurrection has only occurred once, about two thousand years ago. That was on authority of the big boss Themselves.

"You mean Himself."

"Nope, our chief in charge uses They/Them and Their pronouns, since They are every gender. Every down dweller, regardless of how they identify, are made in Their image after all."

"Well, that explains a lot. Not a lot of people down there are aware of that, I'm afraid."

"That's because of widespread ignorance based on misinformation, but again, that's not my department. Now where were we? Oh right, you were asking how to connect with your job assignment. Down dwellers can't see you, but you will be able to reach out to them on other levels. It works differently for everyone, so you are going to have to figure out what works for you. If at any point the job becomes too demanding, we'll reassign you. Luckily, that hardly ever happens. At the Afterlife Agency we only assign jobs we think our employees can handle."

"So, what's my first job?"

"I think it will be right up your ally. You'll be supervising an injured football player who's struggling with mental health issues. The details will be in this letter."

Gabe hands me an envelope.

"Like I said before, if you need a break, or a shoulder to cry on, just close your eyes and say 'Cheeky Rooster'. You'll end up in our world-renowned afterlife pub. I would certainly pop in tonight. Rumour has it that Ms Winehouse and Mr Mercury are performing their first duet."

With that, he turns back to his computer screen, seemingly oblivious to my presence.

Olga gently tugs my arm.

"Come on Calum, I'll show you how to get to your first assignment."

As we leave the job agency, I'm struggling to wrap my head around what just happened.

"Are you alright love? You look a bit pale."

"I'll be alright. Just trying to come to terms with all of it."

"I know it's overwhelming, but don't worry. You'll get the hang of it soon enough."

"Gabe seems to think I'm thick, though."

"Don't mind him. He's like that with every newbie. Call it a rite of passage. I think you've got lots of potential."

"So how do I get to this injured football player? Do I have wings? Can I fly there?"

"Heavens, no, you're not a celestial being. We've got other means of transportation. Look, here we are."

We come to a stop in front of three adjacent elevators. Olga pushes a button, and I hear a soft swooshing sound. The doors of the one in the middle open. Inside there's a panel that roughly resembles a computer's keyboard.

"Have a look at the envelope Gabe gave you, love. There's a password on the front consisting of several numbers, letters, and symbols. Please be careful not to make any mistakes, or you might end up in the wrong place."

My password doesn't seem that complicated. It has four numbers, two letters and a symbol.

"I'll leave you to it then. Good luck Calum."

With that Olga turns around and leaves, before I can throw in so much as a goodbye.

Okay, don't panic Calum, how hard can it be to use an elevator. You've done so countless of times during all of those hospital visits. For a moment, I'm transported back to three years of walking in and out of medical care facilities, getting second opinions and treatments. In the beginning, we'd make a day of it. Having cake and coffee in the hospital cafeteria, watching a movie at the cinema, or going shopping. Mum used to say that these hospital visits weren't for the fun of it, but at least we could make some nice memories. That's when everyone still thought I was going to be okay. I was in the prime of my life, fit as a fiddle, and hellbent on getting better. My body decided otherwise, though. The hardest part was having to let go of everyday life activities. As I got sicker, I couldn't attend classes anymore. In the beginning I would log in online during lectures, my college professors more than willing to oblige. After a while I couldn't keep up anymore. My pain medication made me drowsy and unfocused. My friends and the occasional teacher kept coming over to see how I was doing. They always made sure to leave a load of coursework on my desk. Sadly, I never got around to getting any of it done, but I guess no one really expected me to. On top of that, certain bodily functions became seriously dormant. I had always taken my random hook-ups for granted, glad I wasn't in a relationship. That backfired when I got sick.

Although physical intimacy wasn't in the cards anymore, I had no one to hold my hand, kiss my tears away, or snuggle up to under the covers. Though I had people visit me on a daily basis, I felt lonely. Suddenly, a pre-recorded voice blasting through the elevator brings me back to reality. 'Do you need any help getting where you need to go? Press one for assistance, press two in case of emergency.'

I take a quick look at my envelope and start typing in the code. The doors close and I feel the elevator move. Just as I wonder whether I'll be moving up or down, it moves sideways, then up for a while, sideways again and then down. A ping announces I've arrived at my destination. As I squint my eyes at the bright daylight, I realise I'm looking at an impressive mansion in the countryside. I suppose my client is inside. Should I ring the doorbell? Wait, I have this set of instructions I haven't read yet. Before I do anything else, I take a handwritten letter from the envelope and start reading.

Dear Calum,

First of all, welcome to the Afterlife Agency. We're very happy to have you with us. Your first job concerns a young man called Phillip Brisbane. He's a 21-year-old injured football player struggling with mental health issues. He's benched for at least the rest of the season. Whether he'll ever be able to perform up to his usual standards is still unknown. This is what Mr Brisbane needs:

- *Supportive friends*

- *Career alternatives*

- *Professional help*

Once these requirements are met, your assignment ends. Since this is your debut at our agency, please take note of the following.

Our clients cannot see us, but they can sense our presence. The better we connect with them, the more they'll be aware of us. When you speak to them, you'll be that little voice inside their heads. Be careful though, you don't want your client to think he's going mad. Please feel free to reach out, should you have any questions. Tap this letter twice, say 'Afterlife Agency' and I'll be at your service.

Kind regards,

Gabe Wandsworth
Office Manager
Monday–Eternity
09.00–17.00

Chapter Two

When you've been as sick as I have, you get to see all sorts of medical specialists. I've been examined, x-rayed, and tested to an extend that surpassed my worst expectations. I especially hated wearing those hospital gowns. I always felt they showed way more skin than I wanted to share with anyone other than my occasional hook-ups. After a while, I got used to having every inch of my body prodded and looked at by people I hardly knew. Needless to say I was grateful to all of my doctors for their unwavering efforts of keeping me alive. Yet I hated the feeling of slowly losing control. The worse I got, the more I was left out of everyday decisions concerning my body, health, and general wellbeing. After I got my so-called death sentence, an elderly lady came to visit me twice a week. In the beginning I thought she was a Samaritan, doing charity work for terminally ill patients. She was a psychologist, though, trying to help me make sense of my situation. I didn't talk much at the beginning. What was there to talk about? I was in the prime of my life, had everything going for me, but was dying nonetheless. There was nothing she could say or do to make me feel better about that. So during our first few appointments I mostly sat in silence, while she was making small talk about her life. Her presence was oddly comforting, though. She emanated this soothing vibe that made me feel peacefully at ease. After our fourth session I started telling her about my life. It was more meaningful than chatting with family or friends. We talked and laughed, and when she left, there was this lightness inside my chest I hadn't felt for a long time. Once she told me that someone with my good humoured nature would end up doing well in the afterlife. Surely the universe wouldn't waste the potential of a dashing young man like me. Never knew what to say to that. Of course she meant well, but I didn't really believe in either heaven or hell, despite what they taught me in Sunday school. I always thought that once you were dead, that was literally the end of it. Since I wouldn't be aware of my body slowly decomposing six feet under, the thought of dying didn't bother me much. It bothered me way more that I had to leave my parents behind, undoubtedly inconsolable. Maybe I can take a little trip in one of those elevators and check up on them. I'll ask Gabe or Olga next time I see them.

First, I have a job to do. I briefly skim through my letter again. I should be ecstatic about my first assignment. Helping out an injured football player suits me perfectly. I played select football for years. I vividly remember my try-outs. I had just started secondary school. All the other lads I was competing with seemed older and more skilled than me. Mum said that age didn't matter, and that I should just focus on giving it my all. So I did, and surprisingly made it to the team. We were a tight-knit bunch, mainly because we spend so much time together. During games we were extremely focused and competitive, scolding each other when we messed up. Off the field we were three shots short of a stag do. There was lots of locker room banter and laughter. Coming out to my teammates was as easy as breathing. It helped that our assistant coach was gay too, and by no means in the closet. His boyfriend came to every game and whenever we won, he'd give him a celebratory smooch in front of everyone. I was lucky, though. I know that most sport clubs have a long way to go when it comes to tackling homophobia. I can honestly say I spent the best years of my life in that team.

Unfortunately, things took a turn for the worse when I was about eighteen years old. During practice I was easily out of breath, and couldn't keep up with the rest. First, they thought it was a lingering flu, until it got worse. I couldn't do one lap around the field without nearly collapsing. I had my bloodwork done and was referred to a specialist immediately. From that moment on, my football career ended. In the beginning I still went to training sessions whenever I felt up to it. My coach and teammates were incredibly supportive, although I needed to sit down like every five minutes. I couldn't play games anymore. After about a year, my spot on the team was given to someone else, which I totally understood. It still hurt though, cause it made me realise that things weren't going to get better any time soon. What got me through was my now former teammates. They took me to every game, making sure I had a front-row seat, and that I was comfortable.

When I got to the point that I couldn't leave the house anymore, my team organised a charity match to help my parents cover some of my health care bills. They live-streamed the game, so I could watch it from my bed, my parents at my side. After all that's happened in my short-lived life, I have a pretty thorough understanding of how important it is to be surrounded by people who have your back. This guy Phillip

Brisbane probably hasn't, since he is in need of friends and professional help. I haven't got a clue how to help him get back on his feet, but I will give it my all, just like my family and friends have done for me.

As I walk up to his house, I cannot help but wonder why his name doesn't ring a bell. Having been a fanatic football player and avid fan all my life, I pretty much know everyone who is someone in paid football. Mr Brisbane surely must be someone, cause his mansion is next level posh. Its front lawn is so big, it's roughly the size of three football pitches. Judging by the mansion's façade alone, it's safe to say it's a high end home. I don't bother ringing the bell, but walk right through the door. Another perk of being dead. Olga told me I can walk straight through walls and doors as I please, cause I no longer carry any bodily weight. As I step through Mr Brisbane's substantially thick front door, it feels a bit like walking through a dense fog. My vision is briefly obscured, so I'm glad when I stumble into his entrance hall. What I see is beyond my wildest expectations. There's a split spiral staircase with intricately decorated railings. I'm standing on a white marble floor with an arabesque mosaic tile pattern. Huge glass stained sliding doors are leading to an indoor conservatory. A huge crystal chandelier is dangling from the ceiling. The hall itself looks rather minimalistic, with just a few potted plants here and there. Less is more in this case, cause there are more than enough eye-catchers to feast your eyes on. I wonder if Mr Brisbane is home, so I can try to connect with him. Since it's no use calling out to him, I'll just have a nosey around the house then. As I walk up the stairs it's awfully quiet. He's probably out, but that's okay. At some point he'll come home. Besides, I can wait, I've got eternity after all.

Just as I'm about to walk through a bedroom door, I hear the front door open. I run back to the top of the staircase, obviously dying to know, no pun intended, what my first client looks like. As the door opens, a kid and two teens walk in. I spot a little girl with pigtails, a teenage girl, and a boy close to my age, all dressed in school uniforms.

"Do you think Dad's home?" The kid asks.

"No Maisy, he's with Mum at the hospital. He'll be home for supper," the older girl answers.

"Dad said there are some leftovers in the freezer," the boy adds.

"Hope we're not having lasagna again, not for the third time this week," Maisy sulks.

"How about I'll get you some milk and chocolate chip cookies, Maise? I think we deserve a treat after school. Do you want anything, Randell?"

"No thanks, Debs, think I'll be going upstairs."

"Fine, I'll be taking Maisy to her ballet lesson. Can you pick up Dad tonight?"

"Sure, will do."

I follow Maisy and Debs to the kitchen. Debs whips up two glasses, then fills them to the brim with milk. She opens a cupboard and takes out a plate neatly covered in tinfoil. From their little exchange earlier, I gather that they're siblings. They all have strawberry blond hair, albeit Randell is the only one with curls. On top of that, Debs and Randell have the exact same almond-shaped brown eyes. Maisy has a set of stunning green ones, now looking expectantly at her sister.

"Can we have ice cream for desert?"

"Let's have these cookies first, shall we? Mrs Buchannon baked them last night."

"I hope they're not as dry as her vegan oatmeal cookies from last week."

"Maisy, that's not a very nice thing to say, is it? It's very kind of Mrs Buchannon to look after us like that. Let's try them first."

"These ones taste nice."

"They do. I think we should send her a thank you note. Make sure she'll keep those cookies coming."

Maisy giggles and swallows the rest of her cookie.

"Why don't you go upstairs? You can watch cartoons for a bit. When it's time for ballet, I'll call you downstairs."

After Maisy has run upstairs, Debs takes out her phone and starts texting. A hint of a smile spreads across her face now and then. She has dark circles under her eyes, but when she smiles it lights up her face, and makes her look years younger. After a while she cleans the dishes from the kitchen counter and walks up the stairs. It's quite obvious these kids live here, but why? What is their relation to Philip Brisbane? They can't be his children. He's too young for that. Could Philip be a fourth sibling? One that hasn't come home yet? I might take another look around before I jump to any conclusions. But I have this daunting feeling these kids are left to fend for themselves a lot. Just in case anyone can sense me, I make sure I tread carefully. The first room I walk in is Maisy's. She's on her bed watching Sponge Bob cartoons. On her nightstand is a picture frame. There's a woman in the photo with the exact same green eyes as hers. She too has strawberry blond hair. This must be her mum then. The one who's at the hospital. I hope she's alright and getting better. As I walk into the second bedroom, I spot

Debs sitting at her desk, behind her laptop. She's typing away at what looks like a book report. Every few minutes, she stares into the distance. Then she gives up and closes her laptop. As I'm about to leave she mutters to herself;

"I might as well fail my English literature class, since I'm doing a pretty awesome job of failing at everything else."

She doesn't strike me as the kind of girl to fail at anything to be honest, nor as one to give up easily. I tiptoe to the next room, which happens to be Randell's. He's sitting on a beanbag, latest I-phone in hand. Indie pop is softly playing in the background. My kind of music, though I'd never thought it would be his too. Don't know why, but I'd say he'd be more of a punk rock kind of guy, fighting the establishment while listening to The Stooges or Dead Kennedys. His room is rather minimalistic. There's a guitar in one corner, sheet music carelessly tossed aside. His desk is littered with schoolbooks, and notes hastily scribbled on random pieces of paper. There's a twin bed, sheets pulled back, with a pair of flannel pyjama bottoms half sticking out from under his pillow. There is no TV or music installation in his room. Then again, a laptop and phone will do just fine these days. He hasn't got any posters or pictures on his walls, except for a calendar. It's a custom made one, cause every month has a family picture. Since it's October, this month's picture was taken at Halloween. The entire family is wearing costumes. Maisy is dressed as the cutest butterfly I've ever seen. Debs is dressed as Wednesday, her stoic, unfazed glare uncanny. Mum and Dad are wearing a couple's costume; salt and pepper shakers. Randell is dressed as Ronald Weasley, a bit of a cliché with his ginger locks, but his Gryffindor robes actually look quite good on him. One date is marked on the calendar this month; *Halloween dance with Patricia.* Oh, looks like he's got a date. Good for him, cause he seems a bit moody. Randell is swiping away on his phone. Apparently he's on Tinder too. Quite the Casanova, this one. I know I really shouldn't, but I can't resist taking a cheeky peek at what sort of ladies he's into. Such a handsome young lad, must have the pick of the bunch with them. I crane my neck to look over his shoulder. Wait, that app looks familiar to me. It's not the pink flame logo I expected to see, but it's a black mask with a yellow background. I feel like I've overstepped some serious boundaries, so I retreat as fast as I can.

There can be lots of reasons for Randell to be on Grindr, no need for speculation. Of course that's all I can think about right now, so I'm glad when I hear Deb's voice, calling out to him.

"Randell, can I come in for a moment, please?"

"Sure, door's open."

"Just wondering how you're getting on prepping for you exams."

"I'm fine. Should be easy enough, since I'm repeating last year."

"Yes, but you failed half of your exams back then."

"I will graduate this year, I promise. For goodness' sake, I'm nineteen. Can't wait to move on to college. Last year I wasn't exactly focused. Mum just had her accident, and we were all so worried she wasn't going to make it."

"Not much has changed since then."

"Well, she's alive. There's still hope she's going to wake up one day."

"Do you really believe that?"

"I have to. We can't go on like this forever. Dad's a mess, barely showing his face at work. It's a matter of time before the board steps in and replaces him."

"Wouldn't be such a bad idea if Dad takes it easy for a while. Maybe take a step back."

"He loves his company. He built it from scratch."

"He loves his family more."

"Then he might consider coming home once in a while."

"I'll talk to him when he gets back tonight."

"Thanks. I know things won't go back to how they used to be."

"We did have some great times though, didn't we? I love this picture of us celebrating Halloween. You look adorable as Ron."

"Don't count on me wearing those robes ever again."

"Are you and Patricia wearing a couple's costume this year?"

"As far as she's concerned, we are. She wants us to go as Marvel superheroes, preferably Wonder Woman, and Captain America."

"Wow, fancy seeing you in a suit of armour."

"Yup, my ginger quiff will definitely stand out."

"Well, you know what they say, happy wife, happy life."

"Nope, not for me. Thanks, but no thanks."

"Everything alright? You've been together for nearly three years."

"We're fine. It's just that I'm way too young to think about tying the knot."

"Sure, I'll leave you to your course work then. I'm taking Maisy to ballet and then I'll start on dinner."

After Debs has left, Randell picks up his phone again. He takes a deep breath, sighs and swipes right.

I feel like there's an interesting back story when it comes to Randell, but I shouldn't get involved. Besides, he's not my client. Can't help picturing him in a Captain America costume, though. Ginger hair or not, he would absolutely rock it. Since I can't make my next move till Philip Brisbane returns, I might as well do some more snooping around. I somehow end up in Debs's bedroom again. I really feel for her. She can't be much older than what, fifteen? She's already taken so much on her shoulders. I open her laptop, curious to see what she is working on. It's a half-finished book report, due for today. Oh dear, I'm afraid she's given up on it. But wait, I think I know this story. It's a novel by Oscar Wilde, the Picture of Dorian Gray. It was the only novel I actually enjoyed reading back in school. Just imagine, a friend draws your portrait, and then someone else convinces you that beauty is everything. You sell your soul to the devil, and instead of aging, your portrait does the dirty work for you. I would have loved to have had a stand in when I got sick. I would have stayed strong and healthy while my portrait bore the brunt of my illness. I know things didn't end well for Dorian, but the thought of a loophole really appeals to me. Apart from that, I sympathise with the author. Oscar Wilde was married and had a family, but he liked men, too. He may have been bi, pan or just gay; in those days, none were really an option. He ended up in prison for who he was and died a lonesome death, having lost most of what he held dear. Goes to show that society has come a long way since then, although there's still plenty of room for improvement. You know what? I'm going to finish that report for her. I start typing and not before long, I'm done. I leave the laptop open, so Debs can mail it to her teacher.

Right, Debs and Maisy aren't back from ballet yet, so I might have another look around. As I enter Randell's room, he's not in. He can't be far, cause he left his phone on his beanbag. Then I hear the all too familiar sound of a Grindr notification. I pick up his phone and take a look. I see a picture of a handsome, well-built torso; six-pack and v-cut clearly visible. His name is *out2play*, weirdly enough, that rings a bell. When I was about eighteen and first went on Grindr, I had a match with someone using a similar name. He was called *2canplay*. Come to think of it, the pic looks kind of similar too. I remember, cause he had this tiny tattoo of a ladybug, just over this left hip bone. This guy has a butterfly, but still. Back then I nearly bailed out on him, because I was so nervous. When I got to his place he turned out way older than he had claimed in his text messages. He didn't have a sixpack or v-cut either. Somehow he sweet-talked me into having a drink, so I wouldn't have come all this way for nothing. One drink soon became two and then some more. At this point I didn't bother anymore, and we hooked up. It was everything I hoped my first time wouldn't be, but I can't turn back time. Before I change my mind, I start typing a message.

Hey there, care to video call?

It takes a minute, but then he types back.

I'd rather not, why not leave a little mystery between us till we meet.

Why? So I can drive all the way over, only to discover you're a forty something middle-aged balding man, with a sixpack in the fridge rather than where it should be?

Wow, you're not a very trusting person, are you?

Just don't like any unpleasant surprises.

How about I send you some more info about me.

A few seconds later, a dick pic pops up. No way this is for real. It looks like a copy and paste job from a mediocre porn site. I have to put an end to it. I'm not letting Randell get involved with this creep.

That's quite something Mr out2play. Now that we're sharing, I'd like to share something too.

Yes please, can't wait.

The thing I wanted to share is that I lied about my age. I'm fifteen.

I don't mind, I lied about my age too. Am in my thriving thirties.

Why don't you come over? I live with my dad, but he's never in. He's been working 24/7 lately.

Are you sure?

My dad is the Attorney General, he's always at the office. We won't get caught.

I don't think we should meet.

Come on, you're using a fake name, and fake pics obviously. No way my dad can track you down.

Two seconds later, the block icon appears in the top left corner. Good, hope I scared the crap out of him, and that he'll think twice before catfishing anyone else. I quickly delete all messages and pics and put the phone back on the beanbag. It's like nothing ever happened.

I think it's time to find out more about this Philip Brisbane. After all, he's my client. The more I learn about him, the easier it will be to connect with him. I might as well start by having a look in his room, assuming he lives here. I walk up another flight of stairs straight into the master bedroom. There are pictures of Maisy, Debs, and Randell on the wall. One side of the bed looks like it hasn't been slept in for a long time. The other side of the bed is unmade. Like someone got out in a hurry and forgot to pull the covers back up, tuck the sheets in, and fluff the pillow. Strange, in a house this big and fancy, you'd expect a cleaner to take care of housekeeping. I take a peek in their walk-in closet. One side is obviously for the missus. I expect to see quite a lot of high end designer clothes. This bedroom, no, this entire house breaths privilege, sophistication, and style. Yet most of her clothes are off the rack. I'm not looking at any charity shop purchased items, but most shirts, skirts and jumpers are from Marks & Spencer, Zara and GAP. One item pops out, and that's a Prada bag. I doubt it's ever been used, cause there's still tissue paper around the metal embellishments. There's a vanity table in the walk-in closet littered with eye make-up, perfume bottles and powder boxes. The mirror has a picture taped to it. It's the same woman as in Maisy's picture. She has her arms wrapped around what I assume is her husband. I think he's well into his forties, but his smile gives him a young, boyish look. If this is Brisbane, then he is certainly not twenty-one years old. Then again, the agency could have made a mistake and got it wrong. Weirdly enough, nothing in this house indicates that this man is into football, let alone a professional player. It briefly crosses my mind that Randell might be the athlete of the family, but I quickly toss that idea aside. I'm starting to think I'm at the wrong house. I take the agency's letter from my pocket and look at the elevator code. What if I made a mistake and ended up somewhere else completely? No doubt this family needs some looking after, but that can't be me. A seven-year-old girl, an overworked teen, and a closeted high school senior. I haven't even taken their father into account, who can't be doing well either, judging by what I've heard so far. I'll wait till Dad gets back, just to make sure I know exactly who live here. Then I'll make another trip to the afterlife agency to figure out what's going on. As I make my way downstairs, I hear a door slam. Guess Maisy and Debs are home.

"I'm sorry Maise, Dad's staying with Mum tonight. He'll video call in an hour or so, to read you your favourite bedtime story."

"I don't want to talk to Dad on the phone. He promised he'd be here."

"I know love, but Mum had another episode this afternoon and Dad doesn't want to leave her all alone."

"Will she be alright?"

"She has the best doctors and nurses looking after her. I'll ask Dad if we can visit tomorrow. Tell you what, Randell will be home soon. I'll order takeout and we'll have a pizza and movie night. Looks like we could all do with a distraction."

"Can we watch Frozen?"

"Again? Maise, we know that film by heart."

"I know. That's the best part. Let's do funny voices again. I'll be Elsa, you'll be Anna, and Randell can be Olaf."

"Fine, go get your DVD."

DVD? I haven't seen one of those around for a decade, not with all these streaming services available. Maisy doesn't seem disturbed in the slightest, and is happily bouncing upstairs to get her copy. After a while, I hear her stomping about loudly. When I get to her room, she's still looking. I spot it lying underneath a huge pile of dirty laundry. I slowly and carefully give it a little nudge. It works, cause it's clearly visible now. It doesn't take long for Maisy to notice it, too. Good, movie night is saved. I take out Gabe's letter. I think it's time to go and see him again. There is no Philip Brisbane, at least not here.

Chapter Three

I carefully read Gabe's letter once more. Right, here we go. Travelling in that elevator wasn't so bad, but I have no idea what to expect now. I take a deep breath, tap the letter twice and say 'afterlife agency'. I hear a faint buzzing sound and then the room starts spinning. It's like I'm in those dancing tea cups, without the cheerful music. Just as I wonder whether a dead person can still throw up, the spinning slows down. I open my eyes and stare at the agency's wooden door. I give the door a firm knock and patiently wait to be let in. When I hear no one call, I knock again. Maybe they're in a meeting and haven't heard me knock. I carefully open the door to take a peek inside. The office is deserted except for Gabe. He's still staring daggers at his screen. I scrape my throat to get his attention. When he doesn't respond, I walk up to him.

"Gabe, hi. I knocked, but I guess you didn't hear me."

"Oh, I heard you alright."

"Then why didn't you call me in?"

"Cause we're closed for the day. Do you see anyone else here?"

"Then what are you still doing here?"

"As an office manager, my job is never done. After everyone has left for the day, I have to make sure all loose ends are tied, and no one is behind schedule. That basically means I'm doing everyone else's work on top of mine."

"I'm sorry to disturb you Gabe, it's just that it's a bit of an emergency."

"What is it? Is Mr Brisbane tired of you already?"

"Funny you should say so, cause I don't think there is a Mr Brisbane."

"What do you mean?"

"I arrived at this very fancy mansion. The only people who seem to live there are three kids and their dad. "

"Did you enter the wrong code in the elevator?"

"I don't think so, it wasn't that hard."

"You'd be surprised how many employees still mess up from time to time. Let me check. I can see which codes were used today."

For a minute or so Gabe types away on his computer.

"You took the elevator in the middle? I think you're right. The code you entered was the correct one. I'm going to find out who you ended up with and why. Can you tell me anything more about that family?"

"Well, there is a little girl called Maisy. She likes cartoons and ballet. Then there's this teenage girl called Debs who is really smart, looks after her siblings, and keeps the family together. The oldest sibling is around my age and is called Randell. He's repeating his senior year. Their mum is at the hospital. Apparently she's had an accident of some sorts. Their father is with her most of the time."

"Let me enter those names; Maisy, Debs, and Randell, right? Let me see,…oh my, you ended up with the mum job."

"Sorry?"

"The mum job, in the countryside."

"Okay, but what's a mum job?"

"These poor kids you were with earlier today are in desperate need of a mum figure. Someone to look after them now that their own mother is indisposed. Let me have a look at their background story. Right, here it is. It's the Cavendish family. They live about 50 miles north of London. Dad is the CEO of Cavendish Industries, a very successful construction company. Six months ago his wife got into a car accident. She's been in a coma ever since."

"Is she going to be alright?"

"As an office manager, I get advanced notice before a down dweller arrives in one of our waiting rooms, so I can send someone to pick them up. Her name hasn't popped up anywhere, so I suppose she isn't destined for the afterlife yet."

"But why would they send me there? I'm barely older than Randell."

"Wait, let me see what I can find out."

Gabe spends another few minutes typing and clicking, occasionally frowning at his screen.

"Okay, here's what happened. There's been a glitch in our software programme. The bit that matches employees with clients. I told you this morning our IT department is a mess, ever since Mr Jobs left."

"Can't you ask another genius to help out? How about Einstein? He must have been up here for quite a while."

"Einstein was aware of computers, but never worked with them, besides I'd sooner ask his first wife to help me out. After all, she invented the relativity theory."

"She did?"

"Yep, back in those days, men often took credit for a woman's accomplishments. Mileva was extraordinarily gifted in maths and science. It was widely known they worked together on Einstein's theory. Truth is, she did all the math and connected the dots. Two years after their divorce, he won the Nobel prize. The only credit she got was the prize money he gifted her with. To be honest, that was just alimony long overdue."

"So no Einstein, or his ex-wife. Anyone else you can think of? I know Elon Musk isn't up here yet, but...?

"I doubt he'd be allowed anywhere near our IT department, even if he had been. He's quite the visionary, but he has an extensive track record up here when it comes to let's call it, 'interesting decision making'. Mileva would be happy to meet him, though. She's had a crush on him for ages."

"Well, can't you reassign me? Who's looking after Philip Brisbane?"

"Let me see. No one is right now. Let me assign your name to his case for real this time. Wait, that's weird, it doesn't work."

"Why not?"

"It says right here that you've already connected with your down dwellers. Once that happens, you have to finish the assignment before you can move on to anything else."

"Wait, what? I haven't connected with any of them. I've been in their house for a bit, observing, and finding out if there was any connection to Philip Brisbane. That's it, I haven't said or done a single thing."

Every down dweller has its own log file. Whatever an employee does or says during an assignment is registered in this log. I can have a look if you want?"

"Please."

"Okay, let's see. The Cavendish log states that you connected with Debs when you finished a book report for her."

"Oh, that? That was nothing. She has so much on her plate right now, looking after her siblings. She looked exhausted. I thought I'd help out a bit, so she wouldn't fail her English literature class."

"Very noble of you, Calum, but you intervened and by doing so, you forged a connection."

"Fine, I messed up with Debs, but that's all I did."

"Really? Cause there's another entry in this log file saying that you used Randell's phone to go on Grindr. Seriously Calum?"

"No, I didn't. Well, actually I did, but not for any unsavoury reasons. There was this guy reaching out to Randell, and I decided to see who he was. His pictures were definitely a red flag, so I started chatting with him to find out more. Turned out he was catfishing. What was I supposed to do? Let a closeted nineteen-year-old fall for a creepy older guy who would have taken advantage of him?"

"Be that as it may, you still forged a connection when you decided to come to his rescue. Oh, and then there's that little girl, Maisy, isn't it?"

"What about her?"

"The log says you connected with her, too."

"How? I've barely been in her room."

"It says you helped her find a lost item."

"A what? Wait, you mean that Frozen movie? It was under a pile of laundry. I just gave it a little nudge, so she would find it."

"That little nudge was enough to connect."

"So what do I do now? I'm obviously not equipped to look after a traumatised family, who's barely hanging in there."

"I'm not too happy about it either, but the fact is, I can't reassign you. Nor can I put anyone else on the mum job, since you've already connected with all three of them. I can see if there's a way out of this mess. The fault wasn't yours initially. It may take some time, though. In the meantime, I'd really appreciate it if you could keep an eye on them. Like you said yourself; they're barely hanging in there."

"I don't know if I'd be of any use to them, but I can try. Never thought of myself as a surrogate mum. I'm barely old enough to drink."

"Speaking of which, before you head back, you might want to unwind at our afterlife pub for a bit. Looks like you're in for a bumpy ride."

"I might do just that. Oh, one more thing. Since there are elevators that can take you anywhere down below, would it be alright if I look in on my parents? I'd like to see how they're holding up."

"I'm sorry Calum, that's not possible, I'm afraid. A long time ago, our CEO decided that employees can't be assigned to their family or friends. Nor can they pay them any visits. It would just be too hard and distract us from carrying out our assignments successfully."

"And why does our CEO gets to call all the shots? Isn't there a board of directors who get a vote too?"

"There certainly is a board of advisers, or corporate, as we call them. It's just that our CEO makes all the final calls."

"So we all just have to wait until the ones we left behind show up here at some given point? Let's say in thirty-odd years, I finally get to see my parents again. I'll be worried sick about them in the meantime."

"It won't feel like thirty years. Time works differently up here, remember?"

"I don't care how time works up here. From the second I've arrived, I've done everything you and Olga asked of me, even though nothing here makes any sense. I ask for one thing in return, and it's a no go area. You know what? I quit. You can find someone else to look after the Cavendish family and Philip Brisbane."

"Calum, I really think you should take a break."

"I just did, I quit. Oh, and I'm not leaving this office till you'll let me see my parents."

Gabe gets up, which catches me off guard. I've never seen him leave his chair. He walks up to me and grabs my hand. I'm ready to fight him off if he tries to drag me out by force. He holds on a little tighter, then closes his eyes. Just as I wonder what he's up to, he says, 'Cheeky Rooster', out loud. For the second time today, the room is spinning. I close my eyes and hold on tight. Just as I'm about to lose my balance, Gabe starts talking.

"It's alright Calum, we're here. You can open your eyes now."

I'm in front of a pub. A sign attached to the doorpost says, 'Cheeky Rooster'.

"Interdimensional travel takes some time getting used to. Don't worry, it gets easier."

"What are we doing here?"

"Like I just said, you could really use a break. Our line of work isn't easy, especially when you're new to the game and still processing your own passing. Let's go inside."

The pub isn't that different from what I was used to back home. We head straight to the bar, where a bartender approaches us the second we sit down.

"Well, well, a new face. I haven't seen you around before. Nice to meet you. My name is Jude."

"Oh hi, I'm Calum."

"Since you're new here, first round is on me. What can I get you?"

"A pint, please."

"What can I get you, Gabe?"

"A double espresso, please. Might have to head back to the office later."

"You're working too hard. If you weren't already dead, I'd say your job will be the death of you one day."

"Tell me about it. The office is a mess. Callum got assigned to the wrong client. His first case, can you imagine?"

"Oh dear, that does sound bad. Can't you reassign him?"

"Nope, he forged a connection with a couple of down dwellers. Until I've figured things out, it looks like he's stuck with them."

"Ah well, just give it your best shot. What are they gonna do, fire you?"

"Very funny Jude. Where's your better half, by the way?"

"J-dog? He's in the back, taking inventory."

"Tell him I said hello."

"Will do."

"So," I say while sipping my pint. "Jude and J-dog are together?

"Yep, it's a bit of a love and hate relationship. They can't live with or without each other."

"How so?"

"Ooh, let's say they have a lot of history between them. Speaking of the devil, well, not the actual one, of course. Luci a.k.a. Lucifer is in charge of our re-education programme these days. What I meant to say is, J-dog just walked in."

A guy in cut-off jeans and a rainbow coloured apron is restocking the fridge behind the bar.

"Hey J-dog, how are you?"

"Hi Gabe, can't complain. Jude told me you're three emails away from a proper burn out."

"It's not that bad, well actually it is. It's nothing I can't handle, though."

"You know you can always reach out to the CEO in case of an emergency, right?"

"I know, J-dog, thanks for reminding me. Took him one whole minute to name drop his dad," Gabe whispers in my ear.

"J-dog is the CEO's son?"

"Yep, and he never lets you forget about it."

"Wow, he sounds like a right prat."

"He's not that bad. Works hard, keeps the pub tidy, and is great with costumers. Makes his own wine too."

"He's got a vineyard?"

"Nope, nobody really knows how he does it, but his pinot noir is to die for."

"So you two have met my fashion challenged other half?" Jude says as he saunters over.

"Give it a rest Jude, I love this apron," J-dog retorts.

"There there, love. He's the sensitive one in our marriage, as you can see."

"I have every reason to be. I died for you, remember?"

"Here we go. Are we playing that card again?"

"Fine, anything you want, my dear?"

"We're running low on change in the till."

"Don't you have thirty pieces of silver lying around somewhere?"

"You know perfectly well, I've invested those in your pub, love. Remember that designer wallpaper you insisted on getting? And that maple hardwood floor you begged me to invest in?"

"You're right, dear. I'll dig up some change from the tip jar. Elvis was in yesterday, he always tips generously, bless his heart. No need to worry, I'll save the day as usual."

As J-dog and Jude go about their business, I can't shake the feeling I know these two.

"J-dog and Jude seem oddly familiar. Have they been together for long?"

"They started dating about a millennium ago, broke up a few times, went to couple's therapy, and in the end they got married."

"That J-dog seems to have a bit of a messiah complex, though. Why do you think that is?"

"Cause he used to be one."

"Wait, are you saying that… is he?"

"Yep, the one and only."

"How on earth did he end up with Jude? Isn't he the whole reason J-dog got arrested in the first place?"

"It's more complicated than what those down dwellers chose to write down over the centuries. The department of misinformation is having a hard time setting their story straight."

"So what really happened?"

"In a nutshell? J-dog and Jude were childhood friends. In their late teens they started dating, which wasn't easy back then. They managed to keep their courtship under the radar. J-dog was famous for his lavish dinner parties. During one of those suppers, he had a bit too much of his own pinot noir and ended up snogging Jude's brother James. Jude walked in on them. At that time J-dog was developing a bit of a rap sheet for minor transgressions. Jude sold him out for a pouch of silver."

"He betrayed him with a kiss, right?"

"Yep, leave it to an angry queen to make a scene."

"So how did they end up together after all that drama?"

"After J-dog got arrested, things went from bad to worse. At least the down dwellers got that part right. After his death, our CEO sent him back for about a month to make amends and say goodbye properly."

"Quite a love story."

"Well, it took a number of sessions on Aristotle's couch for them to learn to communicate their feelings constructively, and of course to forgive."

"Gabe, are you talking about J-dog and me?"

"I was telling Calum your love story, how Aristotle got you guys back together."

"True, he did. And Freud basically saved our marriage. Speaking of which, it is our 95th wedding anniversary today. I got J-dog a surprise. Watch this."

As I turn around, two people walk up to an elevated stage in the middle of the pub. It has got considerably busier. In fact, the place is crowded. Jude walks up to the microphone and beckons J-dog to join him.

"Ladies and gentlemen, welcome to the Cheeky Rooster. It is great to see so many familiar faces. Some of you may already know, but today, me and J-dog are celebrating our 95th wedding anniversary. So I asked some friends to perform for the occasion. Please give it up for Ms Winehouse and Mr Mercury!"

The crowd goes absolutely wild. I can't believe my eyes. Two iconic musicians are performing live in front of me. Amy picks up her guitar and starts playing. Together they sing this breath-taking duet I know would have been a number one hit for years down there. When they finish, they perform a few oldies from their own respective set lists. Before I know it, I'm on my feet dancing with everyone else.

"Gabe, this is great. This is the best pub I've ever been to."

"This is probably the only pub you've ever been to where deceased A list musicians perform. Mind you, this doesn't happen every night."

"Thanks for taking me here tonight."

"You're welcome. Just make sure you do this regularly, okay? Don't become a workaholic like me. Helping out down dwellers is a noble cause, but we all need to blow off steam. Again, I'm sorry about your parents."

"It's okay, that's not on you, Gabe. Oh, and until you've figured out that software glitch, I'll be more than happy to keep an eye on that Cavendish family."

"Thanks Calum. Since you've already forged a connection, you don't have to use an elevator to get there. Just close your eyes and say their names."

I close my eyes and picture them one by one. Maisy Cavendish, Debs Cavendish, and Randell Cavendish. As soon as I've said their names, the pub starts spinning. It's time for my first assignment. I'm about to become a mum.

Chapter Four

When the spinning stops, I'm back in front of the Cavendish mansion. The lawn hasn't been mowed for a long time. The grass is at least eight inches tall and weeds are growing freely everywhere. That's odd. I would have expected this sort of place to have a gardener. As I walk back inside, the house is awfully quiet. Looks like the children are off to school. I don't know how long I've been in the Cheeky Rooster, but probably all night. I walk into the kitchen where there's a stack of papers lying on the counter. I feel like I'm crossing a line again, but if I want to be of use to this family, I have to know all the ins and outs. I take a closer look. It's a pile of bills from months ago. Lying next to them are several payment reminders. I can imagine Dad's behind a bit, after spending most of his time at the hospital. I can't do much about these bills, so I walk up to the fridge to see what they're having for tea. There are colourful post-it notes on the door, reminding Debs to pick up everyone's Halloween costumes, Dad to pay the bills, and Randell to pick up two large pumpkins from the garden centre. Wow, Halloween isn't due for another couple of weeks, but they're well on schedule with all the preparations. As I peer inside their fridge, I see it isn't very well stocked. There's a piece of cheddar, half a ham, a carton of expired milk, and a bottle of ketchup. I have an idea, though. I'm about to carry out my first official task as this family's surrogate mum. I grab a post-it note and a pencil, and write down; *Dad, pick up groceries*. It's about time he gets a bit more involved. Right, now that I've carried out my first official task, I can't wait to see what else I can do. I'll take a walk around the house to see if anything needs fixing, cleaning or tidying. I'll start at the top and work my way down. I walk up the impressive staircase and end up in the master bedroom. Just as I'm about to walk in, I hear someone talk.

"I am at my wit's end John, I don't know what to do anymore."

Apparently Dad's at home. I can't hear what's being said on the other end of the line, but it doesn't seem to calm him down.

"I know I should be home more often, but I can't leave Grace alone. She needs me."

Dad's quiet for a couple of minutes, listening to this guy called John.

"I know, I know. Maisy really misses me. I think she'll lose it if I read her one more bed-time story over the phone. Debs is in way over her head. Tries to take over from Grace, something a fifteen-year-old shouldn't have to do. At least Randell is doing fine. He seems more focused on school than last year. Thank goodness he has Patricia to look after him. Don't know where he'd be without his girlfriend. Wait, let me put you on speakerphone, so I can change. Been wearing the same jumper for days."

Dad disappears in the walk-in closet, leaving his phone on the bed.

"What about Cavendish Industries Gareth? Are you going to fight the board's decision to make you step down as CEO?"

"Don't think I've got much fight left in me. Past year has taken its toll."

"Maybe it's for the best. Take a step back, get help for that online problem you've got."

"I don't have a problem, John."

"You do remember why they want you to step down, right?"

"I was caught gambling."

"With company money."

"I was going to pay them back. My life has been hard ever since Grace…

Dad, or Gareth as it turns out, swallows audibly and takes a second before he continues.

"Ever since Grace has been in the hospital, I feel like I'm failing at everything. I'm failing at being a competent CEO, a caring father, and a decent big brother."

"Don't be daft, Gareth, you've got a lot on your mind. For what it's worth, you've been a wonderful father to Maisy, Deborah and Randell. They adore you. You've made Cavendish Industries a roaring success. Losing a bit of money doesn't change any of that."

"It wasn't a bit."

"How much?"

"Two hundred grand."

"What? Oh, Gareth."

"I've been paying them back for a couple of months now. Cut down on expenses at home, had to let the gardener go, and our housekeeper. Debs and Randell have been great, helping out around the house."

"Sounds like you're doing everything you can to make amends."

"The money isn't the only issue. I lost everyone's trust. You should have seen Deb's face when I told her I had to let Tracy and Gus go. As far as she's concerned, they're part of the family."

"Maybe you can rehire them on, once you get back on your feet. I haven't lost faith in you, big bro. Don't be so hard on yourself."

"Thanks John. I have to go now. Kids will be home soon. I promised Maisy to watch that blasted Disney DVD with her. She's had it on repeat for weeks now."

"There're enough online streaming services these days."

"Not in our house, cut backs remember?"

"Right, well, give them all my love, Gareth. I'll talk to you soon."

"Bye John."

Oh my goodness, this explains so much. The dishevelled state of this mansion and its gardens, Maisy watching DVDs on repeat, and Debs taking on way more than she can handle. I hope Gareth is seeking help for his online gambling problem, although it sounds he's still in denial. I can't believe this is a one man, or should I say one mum job. There is so much that needs to be taken care of. Essentially, it all comes down to three major things. First of all, looking after Maisy, Debs and Randell. Secondly, housekeeping and maintaining the grounds. Thirdly, Gareth needs professional help. Right, first things first. The kids won't be home for another hour or so. I think I've come up with an idea to find the funds to pay for the upkeep of this mansion and its grounds. Every estate has a garage or a car park. When I got sick, I spent a lot of time in bed watching shows to pass time. One of my favourite ones was MTV Cribs, a show where famous, successful, but most of all rich celebrities, give you a tour in their well, cribs. I've seen many impressive houses, but what struck me the most were the car parks. Aston Martins, Lamborghinis, Ferraris, Porches and so much more to feast your eyes upon. These cars are worth a small fortune, enough to pay for a housekeeper or gardener for a while. As I walk around the mansion, it doesn't take long before I spot the garage. The light switches on as soon as I step inside. It's a nice garage, but not as impressive as I expected. Gareth drives an Audi for everyday use. There's a BMW, which I think is Grace's car. Then there's a Tesla.

It's a 2023 model 3, according to the owner's manual lying on the bonnet. Quite a price tag too, it's nearly 50.000 quid. If he'd sell that, he could rehire Tracy and Gus. The mansion and grounds would be properly looked after once again. I walk back to the house and into the kitchen. I grab another post-it note and write down; *Sell Tesla, rehire Tracy and Gus.* I stick the note on top of the pile of bills I found earlier. Now it's up to Gareth to make it happen. The clock chimes four, and as if on cue, the front door opens. Maisy, Debs, and Randell are home.

"Dad, we're home," Debs calls out.

"I'll be right down!"

"Come on Maise, let's see how those popsicles I put in the freezer have turned out."

I follow the family into the kitchen. Randell's making tea, while Debs and Maisy are discussing which flavour to try first.

"Afternoon dears," Gareth says as he envelops Maisy in a hug. "How was school?"

"Same as usual," Debs says.

"We're baking ghost biscuits for Halloween," Maisy answers.

"Sounds delicious darling, what costume are you wearing again?"

"I'm going as Elsa, and Debs's going as Anna. Can you go as Olaf, Dad?"

"Don't know pumpkin, think I'll sit this one out. I've got a lot on my mind these days."

"Come on Dad. Halloween will be difficult for all of us this year. It's the first time Mum won't be here," Debs says.

"Perhaps Randell can go as Olaf, dear."

"I have to wear a couple's costume with Patricia. She wants me to go as Captain America."

"Right, of course. Well, I see what I can do, Maise. Won't be easy to get a costume at this short notice."

"I'll be picking up mine and Maisy's this afternoon. I can see what they've got left."

"Ah right, thanks, love."

"Dad, can you drive me to the garden centre? We have two pumpkins to carve out before Saturday, not to mention we haven't even started on decorating the house. Gus used to do most of it, but since he no longer works here, it'll be up to us."

"Randell, I really think we should skip decorating this year."

"Why? Our house has always been a legend around here. Parents and their kids come from miles around to see the Cavendish's haunted house."

"Yes dear, but like you said, Gus isn't here this time and I'm awfully behind with work."

"You're behind with lots of things, Dad. The fridge is near enough empty."

"We could order in tonight?"

"Oh, so we don't have money to pay our bills, but we can order in? Didn't we agree a week ago that we would all pull our weight around here? We even wrote these post-it notes to remind us.

Debs is picking up our costumes. I'm supposed to get the pumpkins, and yours says; pay the bills, and wait, there's another one. It says; *Dad, pick up groceries*. Did you write that one yourself?

"No, I didn't."

"Never mind, it's settled then. Debs is picking up costumes with Maisy, and we're going grocery shopping and pumpkin picking."

"Oh, and Dad," Debs adds. Don't forget to pay the bills, okay? It's bad enough not having Tracy and Gus around, but we don't want to be cut off from electricity and running water, too."

"Don't worry dear, I've got them right here."

As Gareth picks up the stack of bills, he notices the other post-it note I wrote.

"Wait, did any of you write this?"

"What does it say?" Randell asks.

"It says; *Sell Tesla, rehire Tracy and Gus*."

"That's actually a pretty good idea, Dad. We should absolutely do that," Randell says.

"I bought that car a year ago. It was supposed to be your graduation present. It's still yours if you want it."

"Dad, I appreciate the gesture, but I don't really need a car. I'll be going to college locally and I can take a bus or a train. Just sell the car and ask Tracy and Gus to come back. We're all trying our best here, but the house and the grounds are a mess."

"If you're sure, I guess I can sell the Tesla. I'll give Tracy and Gus a call this evening."

"Thanks, Dad. Now Gus can help us turn our place into a haunted house, after all."

"Hold on, he hasn't said he'll come back yet."

"Actually they have Dad," Debs interrupts. "I just texted Tracy and Gus, and they'd be more than happy to help out. They'll start first thing tomorrow, if that's alright with you."

"Tell them, welcome back."

Yes, first mission accomplished. Gareth is selling the car, and Tracy and Gus are coming back. This mum job isn't so tough after all.

"Can we get Mum a costume too? In case she'll wake up before Halloween," Maisy asks.

"Darling, Halloween is this Saturday. I don't think she'll be awake by then. Even if she would, she would need to take it very easy for some time."

Wait, what? Did Gareth just say Halloween is this Saturday? That can't be right. I was here only yesterday and Halloween was still weeks away. How long have I been in the Cheeky Rooster? I take a quick peek on Gareth's phone. It's the 29th of October. Only two days till Halloween. How did I just skip three weeks in one night? But wait, didn't Olga tell me that time works differently up there? What if every time I pop in for a pint, I miss out on weeks down here? Next time I see Gabe, I'll have to ask him about this. Now that I'm officially on the mum job, I don't want to leave them alone for too long. I have a feeling it's going to take everything I've got to accomplish the other two missions.

"We need all day tomorrow to decorate the house and get ready for our Halloween party. So let's get going," Randell says.

With everyone gone, I have some time to reflect on everything that's happened. Gareth seems to be on speaking terms with his children again. It's great to see them rallying together to throw that Halloween party. I do worry about Gareth, though; he does have a lot on his plate. He's about to lose his company, his wife is in a coma, and he has an online gambling addiction. I don't think I can fix the first two, but I can try getting him help for the third. There's very little I know about gambling and addiction. I'm not a social worker or a psychologist. Since I have the house to myself now, I might as well go online and read up on the subject. I walk upstairs to the master bedroom and open Gareth's laptop. What I'm reading is not very reassuring. It says that anyone can develop a gambling addiction regardless of their background or intelligence. Gambling is classified as an addiction when it disrupts your life. That certainly applies to Gareth. He's on the verge of being sacked from his own company. Then they're some myths about gambling. You don't have to gamble every day to be a problem gambler. Another myth is that gambling isn't a problem, if you can afford it. Well, that clearly doesn't make sense. This family is very well off, but Gareth's gambling problem has led to drastic cut-backs, disrupting their daily life considerably. People are known to gamble when they're feeling stressed. Gareth must have had so much stress, with the love of his life being unconscious for months now, running a company, and being there for his three kids. I read that people often lie to hide their gambling activities, risk their job, or close relationships while doing so. Gareth has been caught stealing from his company to enable his gambling addiction, but has owned up to it. On the other hand, I heard him tell John he doesn't think he has a problem. Denial is a very dangerous stage to be in when trying to get back on your feet. I think he needs to get his cravings under control, so he won't easily fall back when he's triggered. It says it helps to join a support group. I grab a pen and write down the number of the closest group I can find. They have physical meetings and online ones, which will come in handy if he's at the hospital. It also says he needs to avoid isolation. Well, he has three kids at home, so that won't be difficult. However, he does spend a lot of time at the hospital, alone. And at night he locks himself up in his study, allegedly to work. That's usually when temptation kicks in. I'm going to keep an eye on him when he's alone, just to make sure he won't slip up.

Right, now that I feel slightly more equipped to help out Gareth, it's time to figure out how to handle the time difference between my current dwellings up there and my assignment down here. I tap my letter twice and say, 'Afterlife Agency'. The spinning isn't so bad this time. I guess I'm getting used to it. I don't bother knocking on the big oak door of the Afterlife agency, but walk right in. Most employees are barely looking up while they're busy typing or making phone calls. I walk up to Gabe's desk. Strange, he isn't there. Maybe he's on a break. Good for him, he rarely seems to take one.

"Calum, how nice to see you again."

I turn around to see Olga in another crisp three-piece suit.

"Oh hi, Olga, good to see you too. How are you?"

"Can't complain. What brings you to the Agency?"

"I was hoping to talk to Gabe."

"So that's why you're waiting at my desk."

"Your desk? This is where Gabe sits, right?"

"Where he used to sit, I'm afraid. He got let go. I'm filling in until they have a permanent solution for this job vacancy."

"Why on earth did they let him go?"

"I'm afraid that information is classified, and to be honest, I don't know for sure. Is there anything I can help you with?"

"Well, I've noticed there's a considerable time difference between up here and down below. I missed out on three weeks when I got back this morning."

"Right, that is a lot to be missing out on. There's a simple solution to avoid this. I take it you've already connected with your assignment?"

"Yes, I have."

"Whenever you're ready to get back down there, just close your eyes and call out your client's name."

"That's what I did."

"What you probably didn't do is name a specific date. For example; *Josh Lewis, February 25th*. That way, you'll get to pick up right where you left off, without a time gab. Be aware that you can't travel further back in time than the last time you visited your down dweller."

"Never thought of that, thanks Olga."

"You're welcome. If you'll excuse me, I have to get back to work. As Gabe may have told you, an office manager's job is never done."

"Yes, speaking of which, do you know where I can find him?"

"Try the Cheeky Rooster."

"Thanks again, and good luck on your job."

As Olga walks over to her desk, I close my eyes and say, 'Cheeky Rooster'. Within moments I'm back where I was last night, drinking pints, and watching two of the world's most amazing singers perform. Although the pub is open, the place looks quite deserted. There's someone behind the bar I've never seen before. Jude and J-dog are nowhere in sight. There's only one man drinking at the bar. I carefully approach him. He seems lost in his own thoughts.

"Ahem, Gabe, it's me, Calum."

"Calum son, fancy seeing you here."

He's slurring his words, and his eyes are unfocused. He's definitely drunk.

"Olga said I might find you here."

"Right, Olga. How is she? Settling in nicely at my desk?"

"Gabe, I'm so sorry. Can you tell me what happened?"

"Nothing much to tell, really. I got fired."

"What for?"

"Wish I'd knew. I received a letter saying that my services as office manager were no longer needed, and that I was being reassigned to client-based tasks. In other words, I got demoted, and will be assigned to a down dweller."

"No explanation whatsoever?"

"Nope, but I'm not surprised. Our CEO works in mysterious ways, but still. Maybe I'm being blamed for all the technical glitches in our software programme. I've been doing so much damage control lately, I hardly got around to doing what I was hired for."

"I don't know what to say, other than that I'm really sorry. Is there anything I can do for you?"

"You could buy me another scotch?"

"How about I'll get you a double espresso? Looks like you could do with one."

"I give a little wave at the bartender."

"So, where are Jude and J-dog?"

"Those two? They never work shifts during daylight. Too busy catching up on their tans, antique shopping, or squabbling like an old married couple."

"Which they are, we celebrated their 95th anniversary only last night."

"True, can't believe it's been that long already."

"Have you ever had anyone special in your life?"

"For a while I did."

"I don't mean to intrude, but you haven't been here as long as Olga, have you?"

"Oh no dear. I was born in 1870 to a physician, and the daughter of a barrister. My life was pretty easygoing, being born in a Victorian middle class family. However, my mum died when I was three. She never recovered from childbirth. Father remarried within a year to an older woman. My step mum wasn't unkind, but didn't really take an interest in me either. I was mostly raised by Mary, my governess. When I was ten, I was sent off to boarding school. It was a big change from what I was used to, but I wasn't homesick, like so many other boys. From the moment I arrived, I made two very dear friends whom I considered to be my family for the rest of my life. After boarding school I went to Oxford to study physiology and medicine. I finished my studies in the early nineteen hundreds, moved back to London, and started working in my father's medical practice."

"And that's when you met the love of your life and married her?"

"No, I had already met the love of my life years before, at boarding school. His name was Andrew, he was the son of a politician. His father was Lord Wandsworth. Andrew wasn't stuck up, though. He was generous, kind, a bit mischievous, but full of life. Back at school, I never dared ask if he felt the same way about me, not wanting to jeopardise our friendship. I did always feel we had chemistry, though. At university we remained close. One night, after a few drinks, we confessed how we truly felt about each other. From that moment on, our friendship grew into something more profound."

"Andrew? So, you're gay."

"Back then, we didn't call it that. In fact, we didn't call it anything, because it was strictly forbidden by law, and frowned upon by society. It was especially precarious for Andrew, since he went into politics. Even the hint of a scandal could ruin his reputation."

"So, you kept your relationship on the down low."

"Yes, one could say so. Whenever we met, we were careful not to raise any suspicion. Andrew's family had a cottage in the countryside that was rarely used. We went there on weekends to spend time together. Andrew had some sort of understanding with the servants, they never raised so much as an eyebrow at us. We felt safe, and loved there."

"That sounds great, so you lived happily ever after?"

"For quite some time, yes. When I was in my mid-thirties, I longed for something more with Andrew than weekend getaways. We started taking risks by seeing each other more frequently in places we shouldn't have. One night, I took him home with me. I had a flat just above my medical practice. My father had retired a few years before. We spent the night together at my place for the first time. It felt so good, not just physically, but emotionally as well. Although we could never live like a married couple, to us our bond felt as holy as matrimony. Sadly, the next morning, it all went south. My father dropped by unexpectedly and walked in on us. Needless to say he wasn't as compliant as Andrew's servants. He gave me no choice. I had to enlist with his majesty's services, and become an army physician. World War one had just broken out, and chances would be considerable, that I'd be sent overseas. Andrew begged me not to go, but I knew father would have ruined us both if I had refused. So I went, and never came home."

"Gabe, I'm so sorry. Can't imagine how Andrew must have felt."

"I didn't know what happened to him for a very long time. As I've said before, our CEO won't let us visit any loved ones we've left behind. One day, right before I was about to be assigned to a new down dweller, Olga took me aside. She told me that Andrew's name had popped up on her waiting room list. I was over the moon with happiness. Finally, we'd be reunited. My happiness was short-lived, though. Olga told me he wasn't going to join the agency, he was sent to a re-education programme."

"Oh no, what could he have possibly done wrong, apart from loving you?"

"Olga managed to fill me in on that. She read his file as soon as she knew he had passed. She told me that when I didn't come home from the war, Andrew was inconsolable. He started drinking and neglected his duties in parliament. One night, he got into a pub brawl. He pulled a knife and stabbed his assailant. The man didn't survive his injuries. Thanks to his father's connections, he didn't end up in prison, but his good name was ruined. He retreated to his family's cottage in the countryside. The one where we had spent so many wonderful weekends. He became a hermit and retired from society altogether. He never went out, nor did he receive any company. One morning, about ten years after my death, Andrew was found by one of the servants. He had gone for a midnight swim, and drowned."

"That's awful, I'm so sorry."

"He drowned in the pond we used to swim in when we were staying at his cottage. The servants found a couple of empty wine bottles, next to his shirt."

"So, have you got any idea when he'll be cleared to join the agency?"

"No, I haven't. After Olga told me we weren't going to be reunited, I begged her to let me see him in the waiting room. All I wanted was a chance to say goodbye, something I never got to do when I enlisted. There was so much left unsaid between us. I just wanted to hold his kind, beautiful face one more time. Tell him I was sorry I went to war, rather than taking my chances, and run off with him."

"You would have been ruined, penniless, and possibly prosecuted."

"True, but we would have faced our fates together. Now we both died miserably and alone."

"I wish there was something I could do to help you."

"That's kind of you, but you already did. You're the first one I shared my story with. It's a relief to finally get this off my chest."

"Will you be alright to take on your next assignment?"

"I'm sure I will be. I've helped dozens of down dwellers before I became the office manager. I reckon I'll remember how things work down there. Speaking of which, shouldn't you be heading back to your family?"

"I should, Halloween is coming up. They're turning their mansion into a haunted house."

"Sounds very festive, but Calum, be careful. Halloween is the only night of the year where those who've passed connect with those who haven't."

"I thought I already had."

"You have, but only superficially. On Halloween, that connection will be stronger than ever."

"Thanks for the heads up. I'll be careful."

After we've said our goodbyes, I head outside. Right, I left them on the 29th, so that's when I want to come back. I close my eyes and say *Maisy, Debs, Randell and Gareth Cavendish, 29th of October*. Once again, my world starts spinning. Before I've properly closed my eyes, I'm back. As I walk up to the house, I take Gabe's letter from my back pocket. He'll be getting assignments from now on, rather than writing them. Out of habit, I have another look. His Victorian cursive handwriting is impressive. As I scan to the end of the letter, I notice he's signed off with Gabe Wandsworth, Andrew's surname.

Chapter Five

As I walk up to the house, the sun has nearly set. Gareth, Debs and Maisy are watching Frozen in the living room. They're on the couch huddled under a big blanket. For a moment, it seems like nothing ever happened. They're like any other family watching a film on a Thursday night. Hot chocolate with little marshmallows on top, and a bowl of popcorn complete an already perfect picture. Until you look closer, that is. Mum's missing, and Randell is nowhere to be seen. Gareth is constantly texting, half hiding his phone under the blanket. Debs yawns noisily before nodding off, her head resting on Maisy's shoulder. Right, I'll check in on Randell for a moment. Normally speaking, I would have knocked before entering anyone's room, but that seems out of the question. Randell is sitting at his desk, behind his laptop. Looks like he's cramming for exams. Let's see what he's working on. Who knows, maybe I can help out, like I did with Debs. Oh look, he's writing a paper on Wars of the Roses. I never excelled in history, to be honest. Only thing I remember about this civil war was that it involved two rivalling families fighting for the throne of England. Both families had the emblem of a rose, one red and the other one white. Luckily Randell seems to know his stuff, cause he's typing away. After half a page, he seems to call it a day. Fair enough, there's always tomorrow to finish up. It's getting late, anyway. Randell picks up his laptop and carries it over to the bed. Quite the dedicated student, he is. This essay must be an important one, looks like he's pulling an all-nighter here. I'm about to take my leave, just as I notice he's not typing anymore. He's staring at his screen, like he's willing his laptop to do the typing all by itself. He's started breathing more heavily. Oh no, I hope he's alright. What if he's asthmatic, and having an attack? I should warn Gareth immediately. No, wait, first I have to make sure I don't leave Randell suffocating. I walk up to him to take a closer look. Poor guy, he's all red in the face. As I happen to glance at his screen, there's nothing about bickering noblemen as I would have expected. In all fairness, I do see two men wrestling, but they're both naked, and seem to have a jolly good time. I can't believe my ignorance. Randell's watching adult videos. I should leave him to it, this is none of my business. Hope he finds the confidence to be his true self one day. He deserves to be happy.

The next morning, everyone is up at the crack of dawn. It's the day before Halloween and it's an absolute madhouse. Tracy and Gus arrive during breakfast. Maisy is ecstatic, throwing her little arms around Tracy, hugging her tightly. Gareth and Randell give Tracy and Gus a couple of firm handshakes, but I can see in their eyes they're equally happy to have them back. Gus and Tracy don't dawdle and get to work immediately. Gareth and Maisy are carving pumpkins, while Randell and Debs are decorating the entrance hall. Around lunch time the grass is cut, and weeds have been removed. Tracy has mopped the floors, dusted the rooms, and is now baking home-made treats for tonight. The carved pumpkins are ready to be put at the front door. A small candle placed in each pumpkin, make their grim, ominous faces look extra spooky.

"Good work everyone. Never thought we'd have a haunted house this year."

"Goes to show Dad, if everyone pitches in, we can get the job done," Debs says.

"Speaking of which, I got another job done, sold the Tesla last night. Somebody will be here shortly to pick it up."

"That's great dad, I'm so happy to have Tracy and Gus back. They're wonderful people, and we couldn't have pulled this off without them."

"So, I'll be in the garage for a bit. Will you kids be okay for a while?"

"We'll be fine, Dad," Randell replies. "Maise and Debs will finish decorating the entrance hall, and I will help Gus make our grounds look spookier than ever before."

Everyone gets back to work. I'm so proud of them. Under difficult circumstances, they've managed to come together as a family to celebrate a holiday that has always been important to them.

I'm curious to see whom Gareth sold the Tesla to, so I follow him to the garage. After about twenty minutes, a man shows up. Gareth seems to know him, cause they're on friendly terms.

"Gareth, old chap, I can see why you want to sell this useless piece of tin. Why don't you get Randell a proper sports car?"

"I don't think he needs one Robbert. He will be going to college locally."

"Nonsense Gareth, a young man in the prime of this life needs a proper set of wheels to impress the ladies with. I remember us cruising around when we got our first car. Wasn't anything fancy back then, but we worked our way up, haven't we?"

"Right, uhm, so you'll be taking the car with you?"

"Sure, I doubt anyone would want to buy it though. I might as well sell it to a junkyard."

"Thanks again for taking the Tesla off my hands, Robbert."

"Don't mention it. That's what friends are for. You've got enough on your plate with Grace being in the hospital. How is she, by the way?"

"Still the same, I'm afraid."

"What a terrible shame. She used to be such a gorgeous girl, full of life. Gareth, you should come to the club sometime soon. You've been pining away here in the middle of nowhere. You need a distraction. Word has it Emmeline Vance is recently divorced, and looking for a bit of fun. You deserve a break from all of this, old chap. Grace would understand."

"Thanks for the invite, but I'm fine, really."

"Suit yourself. You know where to find me."

Robbert gets in the Tesla and drives off, noisily honking the horn all the way down the driveway. What an absolute prat that man. Can't believe the two of them are friends, but I suppose they go a long way back. At least the car is sold. He needs that money to pay Tracy and Gus with. After Robbert has left, Gareth walks up to his study. He starts typing an email to the board of directors of Cavendish Industries, asking them to give him another chance. Good, he's fighting back. His phone rings, and by the look on his face, he's not happy about taking the call.

"Hello, Gareth Cavendish speaking. Oh right. Let me put you on speaker phone. I have my notes right here."

"Mr Cavendish, have you thought about what we've discussed the last time you were visiting your wife?"

"Yes, doctor I have, and the answer is still no. She hasn't deteriorated since her last episode. I have every hope of a full recovery."

"I fully understand your perspective, Mr Cavendish. As I've said before, Mrs Cavendish has been unresponsive for months now. She's sustained substantial and irreversible brain damage. The longer she's in a vegetative state, the less likely it is, she'll wake up."

"Less likely doesn't mean never, doctor."

"What I'm trying to say is that chances of her waking up, let alone making a full recovery, are slim to nothing."

"I'll take any chance she's got, even if it's slim to nothing."

"Mrs Cavendish is on life support, and in the event of another episode, her condition will only worsen."

"Thank you for your input, doctor, but we'll never give up on Grace. She would have done the same for us."

When Gareth hangs up, he looks close to tears. He picks up a picture frame from his nightstand.

"I'm so sorry Grace, it should have been me in the hospital, not you. I was home late, so you had to hurry and pick up the kids. Can't believe the last thing I said to you was; please get some takeout on the way home. I just don't know what to do anymore. I'm way in over my head. Maisy, Debs and Randell have been great, but honestly, I think they're barely hanging in there. Thank goodness we've got Tracy and Gus back. Don't know whose idea it was to sell the Tesla, but I'm sure glad we did."

Gareth opens his laptop again and rubs his eyes. He looks exhausted. He should take a break from work. Just as I'm about to leave, I hear a computer recorded voice; 'please place your bets, winner takes it all.' Wait what? Oh no, he's about to gamble. I can't believe this. He just sold the Tesla to be able to afford to hire Tracy and Gus again. Not to mention that he has begged his own company to give him one more chance. I can't let him do this. Come on, think Calum, think! Wait, didn't I write down the number of a support group somewhere on a post-it note? Right, found it. What now? Slip it under his nose? Stick it on his laptop? I've got a better idea. I carefully grab his phone and dial the number, then I put it on speakerphone. Just as Gareth is about to place his bet, someone picks up the phone.

"Good afternoon, this is Sheila speaking. How may I help you?"

"What? Who is this? What's going on? I haven't called anyone."

"This is Sheila speaking from Gamblers Anonymous."

"Gamblers Anonymous?"

"Yes, we're a support group for people with a gambling problem, or addiction."

"How did you find me?"

"You called me sir. Is there anything I can do for you?"

"Uhm, well, maybe there is. It's just that I've been going through a rough patch lately."

"I'm sorry to hear that, sir."

"Yes, well, as a result, I've been making some poor choices, some of them pertaining to what might be considered as gambling."

"That's a very brave thing to say out loud, sir."

"I don't feel very brave most of the time."

"That's very understandable. You don't have to. Just so you know, you're not the only one struggling with this. If you're interested, we're meeting every Monday at eight."

"My wife is in the hospital. I'm mostly over there."

"That's alright, you can join our meetings online too, although I wouldn't do so on your first time."

"Thanks, Sheila. I'll try to be there on Monday."

"Oh, and sir. If you ever feel the urge to make a, let's say poor choice again, please call us on this number. There's always someone available to listen."

Gareth hangs up, shakes his head, and takes a deep breath. He looks at the bet he was about to place and deletes it. He closes his laptop and takes one more look at his wife's picture.

"Can't believe you're still looking out for me, love. Thank you."

The rest of the evening is quite uneventful, thank goodness. I know I don't need any sleep, but it's still exhausting looking out for everyone, making sure nothing else goes south. Now that everyone's asleep, I briefly consider going for a pint in the Cheeky Rooster. To be honest, I could really do with some quiet and alone time. So far, I've accomplished two out of three missions. Housekeeping and maintenance have been taken care of, and I got Gareth professional help. Now I've got to keep an eye out for Maisy, Debs and Randell. They've been through so much, and who knows what's still to come?

Now that I'm on downtime, I can't stop my mind from wandering. As a kid, Halloween was one of my favourite holidays. Dressing up and eating as many sweets as I wanted. While all my friends dressed up as Spiderman or the Hulk, I wanted to be a Disney princess. That worked out fine, till I turned six. That year I went as Aladdin's Jasmine. I was obsessed with the Disney cartoon, so I badgered Mum until she sewed me a pair of turquoise harem pants and a matching off-the-shoulder top. She even got me an oriental-style rug from a flea market, which I rolled up and dragged along with me all evening. Everything went smoothly, till I ran into some year three blokes from school. They started laughing the moment they spotted me. I didn't understand. Did my top come undone? Were my harem pants stained? When I got home, I told my mum what happened. She said that I shouldn't take any notice, and that they were just jealous. I couldn't shake off the feeling that it was me they were laughing at. A few days later, back at school, I ran into the same lot. 'Oi, Jasmine, where's Aladdin?' Maybe you should go rub a lamp or something.' I couldn't think of a clever comeback, so I laughed it off. Inside, I was dying. From that year on, I wore superhero costumes just like the other boys. No one ever laughed at me again. It took years for me to be comfortable enough to be my true self again. My football team played an important part in that. After every game or practise there was the usual locker room talk. At some point they noticed I never joined in, when it came to talking about girls, romance, and all the firsts that come with that. 'Your time will come, Jones', they used to say. One day after practise when I heard another round of, 'Just wait till it's your turn, Jones', I decided to come out. I told them I couldn't wait for that to happen, but when it did, it wasn't going to be with a girl. The whole locker room went quiet for a full minute. Nobody wanted to speak first. Then Jim Davies, a 6ft.2 menace on the soccer field, turned around, looked at me and said, 'Well

Jonesy, when you start dating, that boy better buckle up. I'm still sore from that tackle at practise. Oh, and don't think we're not going to rate your man just because he doesn't wear lip gloss and heels.' That was the end of it, no crass jokes, no homophobic remarks. We all went about our business as usual. I long for the unconditional support I felt in that locker room that day. For the very first time in my existence, I feel homesick. I really miss those guys.

I am so lost in my thoughts, reminiscing about a life that seems aeons ago, I don't notice sunlight is pouring through the window. I've been sitting on Randell's bean bag all night, enjoying the peace and quiet around me.

"What the heck? Who are you?"

Randell has woken up with a start and is staring right at me. Who is he talking to? Did he have a bad dream or something? I look around, but I'm the only one here. He can't be talking to me. I've been around this family for hours on end, hiding in plain sight. No one's ever noticed me before. They can't see me, unless… Oh no, Gabe warned me about this. It's the 31st of October, Halloween. Connections I've forged with clients will be stronger than ever.

"Uhm, can you see me, Randell?"

"How do you know my name? Who are you?"

"Please don't be alarmed."

As soon as I've said this, I realise how stupid this must sound. Of course he's alarmed. Wouldn't you be, if you woke up with a complete stranger in your bedroom, sitting on your bean bag?

"I'm not going to hurt you, Randell."

Again I messed up, cause that's exactly what he thinks I'm about to do now. He is frantically looking for something he can use as a weapon to force me out of his room. He lunges for his laptop and raises it above his head. This is ridiculous. If he throws his computer at me, it'll just end up on the floor, broken. I have to put a stop to this.

"Come on Randell, please don't. If you shatter that laptop, how are you going to finish your Wars of the Roses essay?"

I might as well keep quiet. Nothing I say seems to be slowing him down. If he makes a proper scene, the whole family will come running in. My entire cover will be blown. Don't know how Debs will take it, if I tell her that I've finished her book report, or that I've helped Maisy find her favourite DVD, or that it was me who suggested Gareth to sell the Tesla and rehire his former staff. Not to mention I called Gamblers Anonymous for him and prevented a relapse just in the nick of time.

"Put the laptop down, Randell, before it gets smashed to smithereens. You'll end up watching those adult videos of yours on a tiny phone screen."

"What did you say to me?"

It's working. Randell is lowering his laptop. I know it's a low blow, but I need to get him to listen to me.

"A nude wrestling match between two buffed dudes is a lot more fun to watch on your laptop. Believe me, I've been there."

"Have you been spying on me?"

"No. Well, actually yes, but not in a creepy way. At least, that's never how I meant it to be. Just give me a chance to explain myself."

"You've got one minute, then I'll scream murder."

Oh my goodness, he's not joking. Better bring my A game.

"Look, I don't even know where to begin, but my name is Calum Jones. I died not too long ago. I've been sent back to look after you and your family, because your mum's in the hospital."

"Sent by who?"

"The Afterlife Agency. It's a job agency where people who have passed away get assigned to a down dweller, I mean someone down here, to help out."

"Who says I need help?"

"I don't know how I got assigned to your family, or why, but I did. Apparently someone up there thought you could use a hand."

"We're doing just fine. We've got staff to help us out."

"Whose idea do you think it was to sell the Tesla and rehire Tracy and Gus?"

"Wait, you wrote that post-it note?"

"Yep."

"What else have you done?"

"Among other things, I helped Debs with her book report and found Maisy's favourite DVD."

"So, let me get this straight. You somehow found out my family's going through a rough time and decided you'd come to our rescue. You snuck into our house, spied on us, interfered in our daily lives for no other reason than your own gratification. Well, congratulations, we seem to do much better already."

"You do seem a bit better. However, my job isn't done until I leave you, Debs and Maisy properly cared for."

"I've given you more than a minute."

"So, you believe me?"

"No, I think you're insane, but I hoped someone would walk in as long as I kept talking to you."

"Randell, please, I'm not finished."

"You are. Dad!!! There's someone in my room, help!!!"

Then several things happen all at once. Gareth comes storming in, followed by Maisy and Debs. I'm lunging at Randell to make him stop screaming. As I clap my hand on his mouth, I fall straight through him. Right, I forgot I carry no bodily weight, and can walk through anything, including Randell.

"Randell, why are you screaming? You woke up the entire house."

"Dad, there's a guy in my room. He's been spying on us."

"Where, has he left?"

"No, he's right next to me, on the bed."

"Darling, there's no one there."

Wait what? Gareth can't see me? How's this possible?

"Randell, are you alright? Did you have another nightmare?"

"I haven't had any nightmares for years, Debs. There was a guy in my room, about my age. He said his name's Calum, and he was sent here to look after us."

Debs and Gareth are exchanging worried glances. Maisy, however, seems to believe him.

"It's okay Randell. I had a friend once, who no one else could see. Her name was Elsa. But then she left, because she had to find her sister in a big castle far away."

"Maise, I don't have an invisible friend. This guy is real. He knows so much about us. He told me he helped you finish your book report, Debs."

"Really? Cause I distinctly remember Vicky helping me out with that, before first period."

"What about that post-it note, Dad, the one that told you to sell the Tesla and rehire Tracy and Gus?"

"I guess I wrote that myself. Must have forgotten that I did."

"So, none of you see him?"

"Son, there is no one here. Perhaps we should cancel Halloween this year. I think we've had a bit too much on our plate this past year."

"Dad, no, we've worked so hard decorating the house, and Tracy and I baked all these extra treats to hand out to visitors coming round tonight."

"I'm sorry, Maisy, but Randell seems unwell."

"Dad, never mind. I think Debs is right. I've been having nightmares lately. Guess this was just a really realistic one."

"Are you sure Randell? I can call Doctor Ahmani-Khan to check up on you. Maybe she can give you a sedative to make you sleep better at night."

"No Dad, I'm fine. I'm Sorry I woke you all up."

"Now that we're up, we might visit Mum, before all the festivities tonight. We can tell her about our haunted house and our costumes this year."

"Yeah, can I bring her some cookies, Dad?"

"You know what, Maise? Let's bring some for the doctors and nurses. As a thank you for taking such good care of Mummy."

Gareth, Maisy and Debs are heading downstairs to get some breakfast. As soon as they've left, Randell sits down on the edge of his bed, cradling his head in his hands.

"Great, I'm going insane."

"You're not going mad, Randell."

"Then I'm probably having a nervous breakdown."

"I don't think so. Look, I was as surprised as you that the others couldn't see me. I've connected with everyone since I've arrived. It doesn't make any sense that only you get to see me."

"Lucky me, I feel very special."

"No reason for that. I'm here for all of you."

"About that, how did you connect with Dad, and why did you tell him to sell the Tesla?"

"I'm not sure I should be telling you this, so please don't freak out."

"No more than I already have."

"Well, your father seems to be in a spot of bother at work. The board of directors is considering asking him to resign his position as CEO."

"I know, I've heard Dad talk to Uncle John on the phone."

"Do you know why they want him to step down?"

"He lost quite a bit of money by making some bad invest-ments."

"Well, that's one way of calling gambling."

"Gambling?"

"Your dad lost two hundred grant of company money to online gambling sites."

"Dad would never do that. That's nothing like him."

"Difficult circumstances, and too much stress, can make people do things they wouldn't do otherwise. It doesn't make your dad a bad person. Just one who's been swamped with everything that's been going on lately. All he needs is a little help to get back on track."

"So, is he back on track?"

"I think so. He's been in touch with Gamblers Anonymous. He's going to one of their meetings."

"Having Mum in the hospital is bad enough, but I don't know what we'd do if Dad ruined us."

"That won't happen, not if I can help it."

"What about me? How did you connect with me? You must have done something really special, since I'm the only one who can see you."

"Well, uhm, I uh kept your room tidy for you."

"Sorry?"

"You're a bit of a slob, Randell. I mean, look around you."

"I've barely got any furniture. Even if I wanted to make a mess of my room, I wouldn't have the stuff to do it with. Why don't you tell me what you did for me?"

"I think I really shouldn't."

"If you want me to trust you, honesty would be a good starting point."

"Okay, so I've noticed you've been on Grindr lately."

"What? No, I have a girlfriend. Patricia and I have been together for nearly three years."

"Randell, I'm not calling you out, nor am I judging you. However, I was in your room before you could see me."

"Fine, I've been snooping around on dating sites, just curious to see what all the fuss is about. I wasn't actually going to do anything there."

"Someone reached out to you. I had a bad feeling about him, so I started a conversation. Turned out he was catfishing. I put him in his place, so he'd leave you alone."

"Are you serious? It's bad enough you went through my phone, but then you actually interfered in my personal life. What's wrong with you?"

"Randell, I speak from experience. If you're still figuring things out, that's fine. It's just that Grindr isn't always a safe place to do so. I don't want you to end up doing something you'll regret later, because I know how that feels."

"You have no idea how I feel. I don't want to see you anywhere near my room ever again, you hear me?"

Before I can say anything else, he's stormed out. It's best not to go after him. He needs his space right now, and I need a break. I close my eyes and say: Cheeky Rooster.

Chapter Six

I am looking forward to seeing Gabe again. I've got so much to tell him since we last spoke. Would be nice to get some advice too. To be honest, I have no idea where to go from here with Randell. Gabe's a veteran when it comes to helping down dwellers, and he's currently back in service. I cannot help but wonder who he's assigned to. It'd be nice to share some of our battle stories over a pint. As I walk into the pub, I notice it's considerably busier than last time. J-dog and Jude are both bartending this evening. Nineties boy band music is blasting through the speakers. I'm having a look around, but Gabe isn't in. He's probably up to his ears in sorting out some poor down dweller's messed up life. I'll bet he gets the hard cases, having so much experience under his belt. I'll just sit at the bar for a bit. Who knows? Maybe he'll show up.

"Hey Jude, how are you?"

"Calum my man, I'm fine. How are you? Rumour has it those little tykes down there are keeping you off the streets."

"They sure do. Listen, do you know if Gabe will be in later?"

"He just started a new assignment. I think he's taking his sweet time getting to know his client."

"I can imagine. Nice music by the way. My mum is into quite a few of these boybands."

"J-dog loves them too. He can't wait to have all of them up here, although most of them aren't due for a visit to our waiting rooms for ages."

"Good to know. Hey listen, I was going to ask Gabe this, but I ran into a bit of a problem down there. I thought maybe you can shed some light on it?"

"Spill the T, Calum."

"It's Halloween down there. Gabe warned me that any connection forged with clients would be stronger than ever. As you might have heard, I got the mum job. Turns out one of my charges can see me, while the others can't. How's that possible?"

"Oh, that's odd. I've heard tales of agency employees being able to invade their clients' dreams, or whisper quietly in their ears on All Hallow's Eve. Down dwellers have never been able to talk to us, let alone see us. You must have forged one hell of a connection with this one."

"No more than I did with the others, as far as I know."

"Maybe this one needs you more than the rest. Look, I'm no expert on dealing with down dwellers, but if I were you, I'd keep my distance tonight. You're stepping on to unchartered territory here. Last thing your client needs is a mental breakdown, cause he thinks he's going mad."

"If I had the slightest hint of Randell going mad, I'd take him to a doctor."

"You can't leave the house or its grounds, didn't Gabe tell you? Just because you are bound to a client doesn't mean you can follow them anywhere you like. Our CEO decided long ago that down dwellers are entitled to a little privacy."

"Thanks for you input Jude, I'll keep my distance for tonight. By tomorrow, he won't be able to hear or see me anymore. He'll probably think he imagined things."

"Right, and you will be able to carry on with the job as usual."

"Speaking of jobs, are you and J-dog working all night?"

"Till midnight, All Hallow's Eve is our date night. I'm taking him down to the library's video archives. I have an understanding with the librarian. She'll let us watch gruesome field battles, and mankind's horrid histories, in exchange for a free pint every time she pops in. Last year we watched the rise and downfall of Jack the Ripper. I don't mean a manmade documentary, but the actual footage of what really went down there."

"No kidding. So who was he?"

"No spoilers Calum, you might want to watch it yourself one day. I'll give you a hint though, it's not that poor Polish barber whom everyone thinks did it. They never caught the real perp, cause a very powerful dynasty provided him with alibis and protected him at all costs."

"Wow, I'll definitely go and check it out sometime."

"Hey, if you're still looking for Gabe, he just walked in."

"Thanks Jude, I'll see you later."

As I walk up to Gabe I can't help thinking about everything the afterlife has to offer. Turns out a lot more than I thought. Gabe seems in deep conversation with another man, so I give them some space until I'm sure it's alright to break in.

"Gabe, how are you? I was hoping to see you tonight."

"Oh, hey Calum, I'm fine, thank you."

Maybe it's just me, but it seems Gabe isn't all that happy to see me. Maybe he's had a rough day. I can only imagine what it's like to be demoted after you've worked your tail off for decades.

"Gabe, you look tired. Can I get you anything?"

"No thank you, I'm only in for a minute or so. Just needed to talk to Mr Christie over here."

"Oh, right. Can I pick your brain for a minute? It won't take long, I promise."

"Sorry Calum, but uhm, I have to be on my way."

"How's your new client? Are you settling in okay?"

"Well, uhm, he is, I mean, they are fine. Not a difficult case, fortunately. It was great seeing you, Calum."

With a final wave he's out the door. That was weird. He was totally avoiding me. Why would he do that? Oh wait, the last time we spoke, he told me about his past with the love of his life, Andrew. Maybe he's embarrassed he shared all that. Next time I'll see him, I've got to let him know his secrets are safe with me. I would never betray his trust by blabbing. It's getting late, so I might as well go back to the Cavendish's. By now, they're probably back from their visit at the hospital. I close my eyes and say; *Gareth, Randell, Debs and Maisy Cavendish, October 31th.* Before I can so much as blink, I'm back at the mansion. Night has fallen. The front of the house looks impressive. A dozen or so carved pumpkins are placed on the steps leading to the front door. Ghosts, witches, ghouls and goblins make the grounds look like the set of a horror movie. Flickering fairy lights in the trees are adding to the spooky vibe. I carefully walk through the front door, hoping Randell won't be in the entrance hall. I hear multiple voices coming from the kitchen. Sounds like the family's holding court over there. I'm going to have to listen in on them from behind a closed door. I don't know what Randell will do if he sees me again. I hear Maisy's high-pitched voice first.

"Can we see Mummy again tomorrow, Dad?"

"Very soon, dear, very soon. The hospital staff loved your cookies Maise, let's bring some more next time."

"Can I bake cupcakes then?"

"Sure honey, speaking of which, are we all set for tonight? Soon enough kids will be banging on our door asking for a treat."

"Sure Dad, I think we've got enough to get us through Halloween and Christmas," Debs says.

"Very well. Let's get changed into our costumes then. Did you manage to get me one, Debs?"

"I did Dad, it's on your bed. Let's go Maise, I'll help you put your dress on."

"So, uhm, Randell, I suppose Patricia's coming round tonight?" Gareth asks casually.

"Maybe, we were supposed to go out tonight, but I told her I'd rather stay in with all that's been going on around here."

"That's very thoughtful of you, but remember you've got a life, too. You don't have to put yours on hold to accommodate our needs all the time."

"I know, but I like being here with you, Maise and Debs tonight. It's our first time without Mum."

"I'll never get used to it. Still feels like she can walk in any minute."

"She would have been impressed by all the decorations."

"And our costumes. I better head upstairs and see what Debs got me. You're going as Captain America, aren't you?"

"Nope, Patricia decided to give my costume to someone else when I cancelled our date. She's still hell bent on going to that party tonight."

"I'm sorry Randell. For what it's worth, I'm glad you're here."

"Hey, why aren't you guys dressed yet?"

Debs and Maisy have returned, both looking stunning. Maisy is dressed as Elsa, her long strawberry blond hair braided to perfection. Debs is wearing an Anna costume, which suits her really well.

"I was just about to head upstairs, dear. You both look amazing, by the way."

"What about you Randell? Think you can dodge a costume just because you bailed out on your girlfriend?"

"What do you mean?"

"I got you one as well. Check your bedroom."

Randell and Gareth disappear upstairs. I've found the perfect hiding place in the entrance hall. There is this alcove just behind the staircase, rather well hidden from view. Randell seems to be in good spirits, even though he cancelled his date. He actually looked a bit relieved, to be honest. I wonder if Patricia will show up later tonight. Before I can let my imagination run wild, Gareth and Randell have returned. I have to clamp my hand over my own mouth to prevent me from laughing out loud. Gareth's in an inflatable Olaf suit. He can barely walk straight in this ridiculously shaped costume. He looks like a three-layered cake with arms and legs sticking out. Maisy loves it though. She throws her arms around Olaf's voluptuous waist and hugs it tightly. Debs and Randell are on the floor in stitches. Once everyone's on their feet again, I notice Randell's costume.

He's dressed as Kristoff, and looks absolutely amazing. He's wearing a tunic over thick pants. A colourful belt is wrapped around his waist, complemented by winter boots in the same colour. Most adorable of all, he's wearing a beanie with a pompom. I don't know how the Captain America costume would have looked on him, but this outfit makes me wish I was still alive more than ever before.

"Guys, let's take our annual Halloween picture."

"Should we do this, Dad? It doesn't feel right now Mum's not here," Randell says.

"I have an idea," Debs jumps in. "There's a gorgeous picture of Mum on that side table. Let's gather round it, so she'll still be in it."

"Who's taking the picture? Patricia used to do that," Maisy says.

I'm briefly tempted to jump from the alcove and shout, 'I'll do it'. That would be silly though, since no one but Randell can see and hear me.

"I'll set a timer on this camera," Gareth says. "Just a moment, please. Yes, all set and ready to go. Let's do this."

It takes a couple of tries, but in the end it works out fine. Moments like these are important. It shows them how resilient they are, despite the heartbreak of not having their mum around. It shows them they can still have a laugh, and be happy, guilt free. Their lives are not on hold, so they might as well make the best of them, together as a family. Suddenly, I am rudely awoken from my thoughts by the doorbell. Looks like Halloween is about to kick off.

All night long, parents with their kids drop by to trick or treat. The haunted house decorations are a big hit. Visitors take their time walking around the grounds, admiring the family's hard work. The Cavendish's are a great success too. Everyone loves their Frozen outfits. Quite a few people ask to have their photo taken with them, to which they willingly oblige. By the end of the evening, most of the treats are gone. Everyone had an amazing time. After Maisy has gone to bed, Debs and Randell are helping Gareth clean the entrance hall. A firm knock on the door stops everyone in their tracks.

"Another visitor? This late?" Debs says.

"We're all out of treats, I'm afraid," Gareth replies.

Randell walks to the door.

"Hi Patricia."

"Hey Randell. I know it's kind of late, but I still wanted to drop by and ask about your night."

"Oh sure, please come in."

Debs and Gareth quickly make themselves scarce, pretending the kitchen is a pigsty that needs tending to right away.

"So Patrice, how was the party?"

"Actually, it was a lot of fun. Tom and I were a big hit wearing our superhero costumes. How about you?"

"My sister picked my costume. We're the cast of Frozen."

"You make a handsome Kristoff."

"Thanks."

"So how are you guys holding up? Couldn't have been easy this year."

"We're fine. Well, obviously we're not, but we managed to put our misery aside for a few hours. It's nice to see that we can still have fun as a family, even though one of us isn't here."

"I'm so sorry Randell, I hope things will look up soon."

"Thanks. Listen, do you maybe want to hang out some other time? I'm pretty beat, to be honest."

"Well, uhm, that's the thing Randell. I've been wanting to talk to you about this for some time. I've been waiting for the right moment, with all that's been going on, but there never seems to be one. I'm really sorry, but I guess I'll just have to come out and say it, anyway."

"Say what?"

"I don't think we should be a couple anymore."

"What? Why? I know I've been a pretty absent boyfriend lately, but I'll do better, I promise. Please give me another chance."

"Randell, you're one of the kindest, and most caring people I know. These past few years have been incredible, and I can only hope you'll let me stay a part of your life. I just feel that maybe we shouldn't see each other romantically anymore."

"Any particular reason for that?"

"I feel that we connect on many levels, except for that part, at least not anymore."

"Right, thanks for your honesty, at least."

"Are you going to be alright?"

"Sure, just give me some time."

"Of course Randell, good night."

"Good night."

I think I'm not the only one who's been eavesdropping, cause the moment Patricia has left, Gareth and Debs barge in.

"Has she left already? Is everything alright?"

"You tell me, Debs, don't pretend you lot weren't listening."

"We didn't mean to overhear your conversation, son, but Patricia's voice kind of carries. Especially this late at night, with the house being all quiet."

"It's fine Dad, I'm going to be okay. I'm heading upstairs now. I'm dead on my feet."

I carefully follow Randell upstairs. The night isn't over yet, so he can still see or hear me. Lucky for me, he leaves his door ajar, so I can catch a glimpse of what he's doing. He's on his phone, busy texting. Right, I hope he's got friends whom he can vent to. He shouldn't keep his emotions all bottled up. After a while, as I think he's about to get ready for bed, he gets up.

"Aren't you coming in? You've been lurking in the shadows all night."

Who is he talking to? Can't be me.

"I'm talking to you Calum. That's your name, right?"

Oh no, he knows I'm here.

"How did you know I was still here?"

"Oh, you thought I didn't hear you stomping around the house?"

"I've been really quiet as far as I know."

"From the moment we came back from the hospital, I knew you were still there. You were listening in on us when we were in the kitchen. After we changed into our costumes, you were hiding in that alcove behind the stairs. Clever spot, but I'm not blind, you know. When Patricia dumped me, you were sitting on the bottom stairs. Did you enjoy the show?"

"Randell, I'm so sorry about that. How are you feeling?"

"How am I feeling? For a few hours tonight, I felt really great, actually. That was short-lived though. Now I feel like crap again. I'm sick and tired of being pushed around like I have no say in anything that's going on in my life."

"It's been a long day. Maybe you should get some rest."

"Maybe I should start making my own decisions for a change."

A Grindr notification sound interrupts our conversation. Randell looks at his phone and then swipes right. He types a few texts, then puts his phone in his pocket.

"I'm going out tonight."

"Wait, what? Where are you going?"

"None of your business. You're not my mum."

"Funny you should say so, cause that is literally my assignment."

"I'm an adult. I don't need looking after."

"I know Randell, but is it so bad to have someone in your life who has your back and is looking out for you?"

"You're barely older than me."

"True, but I know my way around Grindr. I know a red flag when I see one. Let me at least take a look at who you're hooking up with."

"Actually, it's that guy you interfered with earlier."

"What? How's that even possible? He blocked you, and I blocked him."

"I created a new account, went online, found him and swiped right. Thought it would be best if I'd start with a clean slate."

"I told you he's bad news. He was catfishing."

"Didn't get that impression when I talked to him."

"Trust me on this one."

"I think I'd rather trust my own judgement, thank you very much. Oh, and don't wait up for me."

With a final determined stare, he walks out. I can't let him leave. This guy he's about to see preys on young and inexperienced men, and lures them in under false pretences. I can't believe Randell is this naïve.

Then again, he's probably really hurt by everything that's happened, and wants to feel in control for once in his life. This is not the right way to go about it, though. I follow Randell downstairs. I could try to wake up Gareth, but he can't see or hear me. By the time I get him out of bed, his son will be long gone. Randell grabs his keys and coat and heads outside. Wait, he can't go anywhere; Gareth sold the Tesla. Randell walks up to the garage, anyway. Of course, he's taking his mum's car.

"Randell, please listen to me. I understand you want to blow off steam. Can't you sleep on it for one night, though? See how you feel in the morning. If you still want to hook up with this guy, I won't stand in your way, I promise."

"Leave me alone Calum, this is none of your concern."

In a desperate attempt to stop him, I grab his arm. To no avail, however. I forgot I can't touch him. Randell gets behind the wheel while I dive in the back seat. If he insists on leaving, I'm tagging along. As we drive off, I'm trying to think of a way to make him turn around and come to his senses. If he doesn't, I'll just shout in his ear the entire time we're at this guy's place. That will definitely kill the mood. As we're driving through the gates, I suddenly have a sinking feeling in the pit of my stomach. The next moment I'm propelled out of the car, and land on the freshly mowed lawn between a ghoul and some goblins. What the heck just happened? Does Grace's car have high tech James Bond like features, such as an ejection seat? Oh no, wait, didn't Jude mention something about this? I can't leave the grounds, since I'm bound to this family, and apparently all down dwellers deserve a bit of privacy. You've got to be kidding me. How am I supposed to keep Randell out of harm's way if I can't follow him out of these gates? Our CEO must have been out of Their mind, when They gave down dwellers free will. Randell is about to get himself into some serious trouble, and there's nothing I can do about it. Or can I? I have to take this up with a higher authority, cause this is definitely above my pay grade. I close my eyes, and for the second time today I call out 'Cheeky rooster'.

Chapter Seven

This time I know who to talk to. I walk up straight to the bar, looking for a lanky man with dark curly hair.

"Back already? How was Halloween down there?"

"Oh hi Jude, it was fine. I'm looking for J-dog. Is he around?"

"I think he just popped in the back for a moment. Let me get you my better half."

If I am to have any chance of rescuing Randell from the claws of a potential predator, I need to have a word with J-dog. One of his parents is our CEO apparently, so he might be able to put in a good word for me.

"Hey Calum, Jude said you wanted to see me?"

"Yes, well, uhm, sorry to barge in like this, but it's an emergency. One of the down dwellers I'm assigned to got into a bit of a pickle. I have to go after him, to make sure he's alright. I can't though, cause I'm bound to the house and grounds where he lives."

"I'm sorry to hear that, but what has any of this got to do with me?"

"I've been told our CEO makes all the big decisions around here. Rumour has it, you're Their son?"

"So, what if I am?"

"I thought perhaps you could put in a good word for me. Make Them change Their mind about keeping me tied to the house and its grounds."

"Calum, even if I wanted to, which I don't, by the way, it just isn't possible."

"You don't want to help me?"

"Can you imagine what my life would be like if anyone could just walk in and ask me to put in a good word with the CEO? I wouldn't get a moment of peace and quiet. Being assigned to a down dweller is hard work, and doesn't always pay off. That's why you have to stay professional at all times, meaning, don't get involved emotionally. Sounds like you already have, though. You're way too invested. All the agency asks from you is to put your best foot forward in keeping your clients safe. Since down dwellers have a will of their own, you'll never be judged on anything outside your jurisdiction, so to speak."

"I'm sorry you're right. Of course, you don't want to go running to your celestial parent every time someone asks you a favour."

"Running to my celestial parent? You think that's how it works? I haven't heard from Them in nearly two millennia."

"I thought since you're Their son, you must be closer to Them than anyone else here."

"You'd think that, but no. First of all, I don't exactly know how closely related I am to Them. Secondly, there are quite a few stories going round about my conception. Most of them are fake news, but our department of misinformation hasn't been able to refute them all. Every time we think we've got every bogus story covered, new ones emerge. Point is, I don't have our CEO on speed dial. I haven't even met Them. After I died, I ended up in the waiting room, just like you. When Olga picked me up, she brought me straight to an elevator, entered some code, and sent me back down again.

A little over a month after, I was sent back up here once more, where I ended up with the agency. My first and only assignment so far has been managing the Cheeky Rooster with Jude. I couldn't have done it without him."

"Right I understand. Sorry if I made you feel like I wanted to take advantage of your connections."

"I'm not sure I even have any noteworthy connections. That's the weirdest part. Growing up in a small town in Galilee, I discovered at an early age, I had powers other people didn't. My parents called it divine intervention, but I don't know. Never felt any different from anyone else. Tried to help out people as much as I could, whilst trying to get everyone to live their best lives. Didn't do me any favours in the end."

"It must have been awful getting arrested, after all you did."

"To be honest, I partly brought it on myself. Should have never hooked-up with Jude's brother James. I was letting my hair down at one of my legendary dinner parties, and got carried away. Jude and I were on a break at the time, so I thought it didn't really matter. As it turned out, it mattered a lot."

"Eventually you two managed to pick up, where you left off. That's impressive seeing everything that's happened."

"We did, but that literally took more than a millennium. We both had a lot to work through. Thank goodness, the ancient Greeks are not only great philosophers. That Aristotle guy really helped us through a rough patch. Freud isn't half bad either. Can't believe one dinner party, or last supper as they call it down below, can cause such a stir."

"Life down there seems so much more complicated than up here."

"True, but it's worth living, nonetheless. Listen, I know you are worried about that down dweller you're assigned to. Have a little faith, though. The fact that he can see and hear you means you must have forged an exceptional bond. He'll land on his feet."

"Everyone keeps saying that, but I'm still seriously worked up about all of this."

"It's called the mum job for a reason, Calum."

Just as I'm about to head back to the Cavendish mansion, Gabe walks in. We catch each other's eye simultaneously. Good, I finally get to smooth things over with him. Or not, cause as soon as he sees me, he turns on his heel, and walks out. What on earth is this? He ghosted me. What have I done wrong? I briefly consider going after him, but I have to choose my battles here. I have to get back down there, in case Randell comes home. I close my eyes and say; *Randell Cavendish, 31ˢᵗ of October.*

The house is dark upon my return. Everyone's out for the count, unaware of Randell's absence. I've been so preoccupied with him, I feel like I've neglected the rest of the family. I check in on Maisy first. She's fast asleep under the covers. The tip of her braid is sticking out from underneath the bedsheets. Her DVD copy of Frozen is resting on her pillow, next to a soft toy of Olaf. I can't imagine what she's been through these past few months. She must really miss her mum. I wish I could go to the hospital and visit Grace. See how she's doing. Maybe whisper in her ear that she's incredibly loved, and that her family is being looked after. What I've heard the doctor say about her medical condition doesn't give me much hope. She has been in a vegetative state for months now, with irreversible brain damage. Even if she were to wake up, the kids would never have the same mum back they once knew. As for their father, I really hope he'll get his life back on track. Whether he'll keep his job is yet to be seen, but what's more important, he's got to be there for his family. I understand he's grieving for his wife, but so are his children.

They need to find a way to get through this together. They did very well at Halloween today, but that was a cause for celebration and fun. I wonder if Gareth knows how much Randell is struggling with his identity, or that Debs is in way over her head, trying to stand in for her mum. I check in on Debs, who's fast asleep. Taped to her wall is last year's Halloween family picture. It was a great idea to include Grace this year, albeit in a picture frame. No matter what, she'll always be a part of their family.

Last but not least I check in on Gareth. His inflatable Olaf costume lies deflated in a corner of the room. His laptop is still open. I take a quick look, hoping he hasn't been on any gambling sites while I was at the Cheeky Rooster. His laptop, however, is showing an online photo album. I click on the first picture. Grace pops up, looking radiant in a stunning wedding dress. Gareth's wearing a three-piece suit, looking equally mesmerising. Their faces look carefree and full of bliss. Newly weds about to start a new journey together, hoping for a long and happy life. It's a good thing down dwellers don't know what the future holds for them. If I had known at the age of eleven, I wasn't going to get past twenty-one, I might not have made an effort at school. I probably wouldn't have tried out for my club's selection team, missing out on what I now consider to be the best years of my life. Being cut short in life is never easy, nor fair. So maybe we're just meant to live our best lives, looking after ourselves and those around us, leaving no one behind. At least, for as long as we can.

I walk up to Randell's room. He hasn't come home yet, so I sit down on his beanbag, trying to think of anything else than his Grindr hook-up. I fail miserably, cause I'm worried sick about him. I have no idea where he is, whether he'll come home at all, and why, for heaven's sake, I let him go in the first place. I wish there was some kind of down dweller's handbook in which you can look up things in case of an emergency. It would certainly have a chapter titled *what to do when a closeted young man ignores red flags on Grindr.* Instead, I'm left with my own troubled thoughts soon spiralling out of control. I can't lose Randell. It would destroy his family if anything were to happen to him. I can't imagine anyone wanting to hurt this smart, sweet, kind-hearted person, but you never know. If he's not back in five minutes, I'm waking up Gareth. No, I'm waking up the whole house. I'll just activate the fire alarm and send everyone flying from their beds. Soon enough, they'll notice Randell isn't here and they'll go looking for him. On second thought, that might not be such a great idea after all. If they notice Randell isn't here during my so-called fire drill, it could cause an even bigger scene. There's just no getting it right. I can't believe I have to sit here, not knowing where he is, or how he's doing, or when he's coming home. I'm losing my mind here. Is this how all parents feel when they worry about their kids? This must have been how my mum felt all those years, when I snuck out of the house for a hook-up. I would never tell my parents when I was seeing someone, but of course they'd already know. Once, my mum left me a box of condoms on my nightstand. On the side, she scribbled *be safe*. Apart from that, she never called me out, or demand I'd explain my actions. I've come to realise that looking after kids is not the hardest part, but letting them grow up on their own terms is. Footsteps on the stairs hurl me back to reality. As I get up from the beanbag, I propel myself through the door. It's Randell, he's come home.

"Where the fuck have you been all night?"

It's a good thing only Randell can hear me, cause I'm screaming at the top of my lungs at him. Randell doesn't respond as he walks into his room. Oh no, I forgot, Halloween is over. It's well past midnight, so it's the 1st of November. Our special Hallow's Eve connection is gone. I follow him into the room, nonetheless. Maybe I can find out what he's been up to by going through his phone. Randell tosses his coat on the floor. He looks exhausted, nope exhausted isn't the right word. He looks sad, and dare I say ashamed? I've seen that look before. Each time I looked in the mirror, after a hook-up didn't turn out the way I hoped for. As he sits down to take off his shoes, he winces. He doesn't bother to take off the rest of his clothes. He crawls under the covers in what looks like a foetal position. I can't believe I'm doing this, but I crawl onto the bed and sit down next to him. I wish I could put my arm around him, telling him everything's going to be alright.

I'd love to tell him that one bad date doesn't set a precedent for the rest of his life. That he's a great guy who has a lot going for him, and that he should never settle for anything less than he deserves, which is everything. Instead, I just sit there, knees pulled up to my chest, hugging myself.

"You were right all along."

Wait, what? Is Randell talking in his sleep? Cause no one else is here. Hope he's not having any nightmares.

"I should have never gone over there."

He's definitely talking in his sleep, berating himself for what he's done.

"I'm sorry I didn't listen to you, Calum."

"Randell, can you hear me?"

"Pretty hard to ignore your little tantrum when I got home."

Randell has turned over and is now facing me.

"I didn't realise you could still see or hear me. I was told it was a one-night thing, because of Halloween."

"Lucky me. I get to be haunted for a little while longer."

"Randell, I was so worried. Are you alright?"

"Could have been better, to be honest."

"Do you want to tell me what happened tonight?"

"Not much to tell, except you were right to assume my date was catfishing."

"I'm so sorry. I tried to tag along, but I can't leave these grounds."

"I thought so as much. When you suddenly disappeared from the back seat of the car, I assumed you'd given up. It was a relief, to be honest. For once, I was free to do as I pleased, rather than having to take anyone else's feelings into account. As I got closer to my date, I started to get nervous, but I ignored it. Suppose I didn't want to lose face, after all the fuss I kicked up. At first, my date didn't start out that bad. He did look a lot older than in the photos, but then again, who doesn't use a filter these days. We started talking, and he seemed genuinely interested in getting to know me. He kept trying to get me to drink wine, though. I knew I had to drive back, so I declined. Felt bad about killing the vibe, so I agreed to take the party into the bedroom. I said I was new to all of this, but he told me not to worry. I don't even remember how I ended up doing way more than I wanted to, but I did."

"Did he ever ask at any point during the hook-up how you were doing?"

"No, not really, but in all fairness, I never told him to stop, either. I was so embarrassed about this situation I got myself into, I just didn't know how to get myself out."

"So, how did you get out?"

"After he was done, he suggested a second round. I knew I couldn't take any more, so I told him I had school early in the morning. Before he realised it was a Sunday, I had grabbed my coat and all but ran out. First thing I did as I sat in my car was delete my Grindr account."

"Randell, I'm so sorry you had to find out the hard way that this guy was bad news. Wish I could have done more for you."

"You tried to warn me multiple times. This is all on me."

"Just so you know, one bad experience doesn't determine the rest of your love life."

"I'm done with dating for a while. I got dumped and cat-fished on the same night."

"Patricia seemed like a really nice girl."

"She is, but she was right about us. We connect on so many levels, except romantically."

"How long have you been questioning your orientation?"

"Since I hit puberty, so for quite a while now. Thought it would be a phase. Then I met Patrice, and we hit it off so well. I talked myself into believing we were in it for the long haul."

"It's okay. Sometimes these things take time. Realising who you are, and more importantly, coming to terms with that."

"I think I'm okay with who I am. It's just been a madhouse around here, ever since Mum's been in the hospital."

"I get it. Hope you'll get some peace and quiet to process other feelings besides the ones you've had about your mum's accident. Listen, I know I can't undo what you've been through tonight, but I can make you some comfort food. How about some hot chocolate, with those little marshmallows on top?"

"Can you do that? You fell right through me when you grabbed my arm earlier tonight."

"I don't know why, but I can touch anything, except for the living."

As we walk downstairs, I wonder how Randell is really doing. He's been through hell and back tonight. First, his girlfriend breaks up with him, and then his Grindr hook-up turns out to be as bad as I feared. It's a good thing he's opening up to me, though. I'm glad our connection hasn't faded yet. I have a feeling he needs me more than ever. I get to work on brewing that hot chocolate. If anyone were to walk in right now, they'd see a pan, a carton of milk, and a tin of powdered cocoa floating about. Luckily, it's still early in the morning. After all the Halloween festivities, I don't expect anyone to come downstairs for a late-night snack. I bring a mug of hot steaming chocolate to the kitchen table. As Randell sits down, he winces again. He wraps his hands around the mug, looking intently at the little marshmallows on top.

"Randell, are you in pain?"

He turns a crimson shade of red and lowers his head even more. The tip of his nose is nearly touching his drink.

"It's okay. You don't need to be embarrassed. It can hurt pretty bad at first. Especially when you're not prepared, or really on board with what you're doing."

"It's just that, uhm, I didn't know what do to when we were in his bedroom, so I just followed his lead. I didn't really enjoy any of it."

"When you're with the right person, you will. It takes time to trust someone, to get to know a person well enough to feel comfortable sharing that kind of physical intimacy. When you move things along at your own pace, rather than following someone else's lead, it'll be worth the wait."

"You're awfully wise for such a young bloke. You are young, aren't you?"

"Yes, I'm twenty-one. Forever, I'm afraid."

"Would you like to tell me what happened?"

"In a nutshell, I got sick when I was eighteen. I received extensive treatment from a plethora of doctors, medical specialists, and other care workers, until I was twenty-one. That's when they told me I wasn't going to get better."

"Calum, I am so sorry. That must have been awful. You had your whole life ahead of you."

"Those last few months I took comfort in looking back on a life well lived, rather than mourning what I was going to miss out on."

"Still, it is not fair."

"Maybe it's not meant to be fair. Life and death are part of our human existence, whether we like it or not. We don't get to choose how long we've got. If we're lucky enough, we get to have a say in how we live our lives."

"So, what happened after you died? I mean, how did you end up here?"

"I was sent here by accident."

"What do you mean?"

"I was assigned to look after a Mr Brisbane, but somehow I ended up here. Even though I didn't mean to, I've somehow forged connections with you, your dad, Debs and Maisy. As a result, the job is mine now."

"And you can only speak to me?"

"Yep, so far you're the only one who can see or hear me. Not that this stopped you from ignoring me when I told you to pull over."

"I know. I should have listened."

"Look, it's really late, or early, depending on how you look at it. So why don't you get some rest?"

"Will you stay with me tonight?"

"Sure, I'll, uhm, keep an eye on you."

As Randell gets up I notice a bit of residual chocolate milk on his face. I walk up to him without thinking and wipe it off with the thumb of my hand. Randell looks at me weirdly.

"I thought you couldn't touch me."

"I couldn't, up till now. I don't know what changed."

"Right, I'm going upstairs to change."

When Randell returns from the bathroom he's wearing the most adorable Spiderman PJs I've ever seen. I can't help but giggle when he walks in.

"I know, I look ridiculous, but we're a bit behind on laundry, I'm afraid."

"Where did you get these in your size?"

"Debs got them for me. It was Maisy's birthday a couple of weeks ago. She felt sad about having to celebrate it without Mum. Debs came up with the idea of throwing a pyjama party, and watch her favourite Disney films all night, while eating snacks for tea. Debs got everyone a pair of superhero PJs. You should have seen my dad as the Incredible Hulk."

"Right then, in you go, Mr Spiderman. It's time to catch some z's."

"You can sleep next to me if you want. It was nice to have you with me on the bed when I got home."

"I don't need any sleep, a perk of being dead, I suppose. I can keep you company though, till you doze off."

"Thanks Calum."

Randel rolls over to his side, his back turned my way. I carefully curl up next to him like a big spoon watching over the little one.

"Is this okay, Randell?"

He nods, while slowly backing into me. I carefully wrap my arm around him.

"Are you okay with this?"

Again Randell nods, while simultaneously yawning.

"Oh, one more thing, Randell," I whisper in his ear.

"What?"

"If you ever have me worried sick again, I guarantee you won't be sitting comfortably for an entirely different reason."

"Okay, Calum."

Seriously? Wow, I'm getting good at this mum job.

Chapter Eight

I wake up with my arms wrapped around Randell. Only a day ago, I couldn't even touch him. On top of that I dozed off, which is weird for someone who doesn't need any sleep. I make a mental note to ask Gabe about these recent developments. I'll go back to the Cheeky Rooster later today, but this time I won't let him ghost me. I slip out of bed carefully, as not to wake him up. He is sound asleep and looks more at ease than I've ever seen him. As I walk into the kitchen, Debs is at the stove making breakfast. The smell of bacon and scrambled eggs makes my mouth water. I don't need any nourishment, but Debs's cooking triggers memories of my dad's Sunday morning full English fry up. He would pull out all the stops, making sure we wouldn't feel peckish till lunch. I was always grateful to dig in, since most Sunday mornings I was ravenous after going out with the lads the night before. When we'd win a match that day, we'd celebrate by letting our hair down big time. To make sure we wouldn't get into any serious trouble, we'd take turns in being the designated driver. Ironically, we never drove anywhere, since our favourite pub was merely a short walk from where we'd meet up. However, after a pub brawl involving my team mate Jim Davies, we decided it'd be best if one of us would keep a good head on his shoulders, just in case.

Thinking of Jim brings a smile to my face. He was the only straight guy I've ever had a crush on. His impressive height, muscular physique, and mischievous smile would make him stand out in any crowd. He was a beast on the field, inflicting lumps, bruises, and sprains regularly on anyone standing in his way. No surprise there, Jim was the most reprimanded player of our team. He wasn't mean, though. He always helped someone up after a full on collision, asking them if they were alright. On and off the pitch, Jim and I had this back-and-forth banter that I sorely miss. Jim was heavy build, strong, and would actively seek confrontation wherever possible. I had a slim physique, was a tactical player, and a fast runner. Needless to say we played different positions, but somehow he always managed to seek me out during a match. He loved sneaking up on me, then shout at the top of his voice 'Oi Jonesy, are you still sore from last night? It's one leg in front of the other mate, the ball isn't going to just roll your way.' Then he'd wink at me, slap my ass, and move on to his next target. Back in the locker room I usually got back at him, mercilessly mocking the injuries he would undoubtedly sustain during any match or practise. Jim was a ladies' man, unfortunately, but not in a toxic way. He'd brag about all the girls who fancied him, in spite of being faithful to the girl he'd been dating since eighth grade. He would occasionally flirt with someone, but at the slightest hint she was in for more, he'd tell her the missus wouldn't be happy about it. One night we were particularly boisterous, after narrowly beating an up till then undefeated team. We were all drinking, alternating pints with tequila shots. At some point,

Jim and I had to use the loo at the same time, so we went to the restroom together, giggling like besties. After we finished doing our business, we heard hushed voices coming from one of the stalls. We didn't want to listen in, but they got louder. Some girl was pleading with a guy to stop doing whatever he was doing. The guy told her not to be a buzz kill. The girl said she wanted to go back to her friends, to which the guy replied; 'when I'm finished'. Jim knocked on the stall door and asked if everything was alright. The guy told him to get lost. One look at Jim's face told me he had no intention of doing so. In fact, he told the girl to stand back as much as she could, after which he kicked in the door. He pulled the guy out by the scruff of his neck. I escorted the girl back upstairs and made sure she was reunited with her friends. Jim's heroic act backfired against all odds, cause the pub owner walked in on their heated argument, and decided to kick out both of them, mistaking the altercation for a drunk pub brawl. From that night on we agreed one of us should stay sober at all times. I wonder if Jim ever knew I had a crush on him. If he did, he never let that on. He treated me like everyone else; which suited me just fine.

My daydreaming is rudely interrupted by the rest of the family walking in. As soon as Randell sees me, he gives me the tiniest of winks of acknowledgement.

It's nice listening to Maisy chatter about last night's festivities, while Gareth, Debs and Randell are comparing notes on the spookiest trick or treat costumes. After breakfast, Gareth, Debs and Maisy leave for the hospital to visit Grace. Randell tells his family he's going to get a start on removing Halloween decorations from the grounds, to save Gus some time on Monday morning. As soon as everyone's left, I catch up with him.

"Morning Randell. Did you sleep well?"

"As a matter of fact, I did. Thanks for staying with me last night."

"You think I'm going to let you out of my sight after all the havoc you wrecked?"

"Probably not. I don't mind, as long as you give me a hand with those decorative ghouls in that tree. I have no idea how Gus got them all the way up there in the first place."

I've never had the upper body strength to climb a tree, but somehow I can pull myself up as if I weigh nothing. Within minutes, I've removed every ghoul and ghost within sight. As I climb down again, Randell is sitting on the lawn, legs folded underneath him.

"So, how's your back doing? Still sore?"

"My back? It's fine, but my backside is much better than last night, if that's what you mean."

"I don't mean to make you share anything you're not comfortable with."

"I know. I've been thinking about what you said last night, and you're right. One day, I hope to be with the right person. Someone who's willing to get to know me first. Until that happy moment arrives, I'm steering clear from Grindr hook-ups and one-night stands."

"Good for you. You're worth so much more, Randell. It still bugs me he just assumed you'd be okay with everything he did. Did you guys use protection?"

"He said he was all out, but luckily I brought some."

"Thank goodness, think I would have lost my cool if you'd told me you let him bareback you."

"Lose your cool? Opposed to being poised and together when I got home last night?"

"Think I could have handled that with a bit more tact."

"Well, as far as surrogate mums go, you're pretty committed to the job."

"I'll do anything I can to help you guys get through this nightmare."

"Thanks Calum. I think Debs and Maisy are doing much better, now that we have Tracy and Gus back. Dad seems in a better mood as well."

"Keep an eye on him, though. Addiction isn't something that goes away the minute you accept help. He has his first support group meeting tomorrow night."

"Don't worry, I'll drive him there myself if I have to. Since you're all about helping us out, how about giving me a hand with my schoolwork? Know anything about War of the Roses?"

"Nope, nothing. I'm afraid you're going to have to figure that one out on your own. Speaking of which, I might pop out for a bit to run an errand elsewhere. Will you be okay?"

"Sure. Will I see you later today?"

"Absolutely. Can't wait to hear how that war ends. You can give me a full rundown of all the backstabbing and betrayal when I get back.

"Won't be worse than an average day in high school, but still. I'll make it worth your while."

I extend my arm so Randell can grab my hand. As I pull him up to his feet, I notice how soft and warm it feels. Randell holds on to my hand longer than strictly necessary. It's like we've just met for the first time, and are shaking hands to make our acquaintance. Randell is the first one to let go.

"Well, uhm, I better get to work then. I've got ancient grudges to disentangle."

"See you in a bit, Randell."

I wait till Randall is out of sight before I close my eyes. The spinning doesn't bother me anymore. It's like riding a rollercoaster in the dark. All I can think about is seeing Gabe when I call out 'Cheeky Rooster'.

As I make my way over to the bar, Gabe is nowhere in sight. It's probably daytime up here, cause Jude and J-dog are nowhere to be seen. The pub is pretty deserted. At a corner table I spot a man in a Cuban-collared shirt, wide-legged pleated trousers, a blouson jacket, and what look like slip-on loafers. He sort of reminds me of a character from one of those fifties sitcoms my mum used to watch. He catches me staring at him and raises his glass in a toast. When he's finished his drink, he walks over to the bar.

"Howdy slick, can I get you a beverage? You look mighty thirsty."

It takes a few seconds before I register his southern accent.

"Oh, hi. Yes, well, uh, I'll take a pint, please."

"So, what are you doing up here, son? Taking a break from your down dweller? Don't blame you. Some of them are lower than a snake's belly in a wagon rut."

"Actually, I quite like my down dwellers. They're going through a pretty rough time."

"Ain't they all, son? My charge is madder than a wet panther. I'll tell ya that."

"I'm sorry, they're what?"

"She's in a horn tossing mood most of the time."

"I'm not sure what that means, either."

"It means that she's a mediocre singer playing gigs for change, and drunk as Cooter Brown on most nights."

"Right, so you're looking after an artist?"

"Well, that's one way to describe her, but yes. Suppose she is."

"I'm looking after a family; three kids and their dad. Their mums in a coma."

"Sounds like they really got the short end of the stick, bless their hearts."

"So, have you been up here long?"

"I've been up here forever. Well, at least since the late seventies."

"Wow, that's quite a long time. What did you do down there?"

"I was a small town country singer."

"Played any good gigs?"

"Suppose so, but I never toured the world. Graceland was, and always will be, my home sweet home."

"Graceland? Wait what, you're Elvis? Thought you looked familiar. Wow, can't believe I'm having a beer with the King of Rock & Roll."

"Don't know what I did to deserve that praise, but it dills my pickle. Haven't played for ages though. At least not in front of an audience."

"Don't you ever miss it? The fame and fortune?"

"Well, that's all temporary, son. I had a great run down there, but it wasn't all sunshine and rainbows. There's a time and place for everything. I'm helping out down dwellers now, mostly singers, and performers who are about to hit rock bottom. After this case, I might just apply for a desk job though."

"You're still very popular down there."

"Some people claim I'm still alive, that I'm hiding out on some deserted island. The department of misinformation and fake news is still working on setting that one straight."

"I can imagine."

"Well, son, I have to get back down there. I left my charge sick as a dawg from day drinking."

Before he leaves, he solemnly shakes my hand.

"Good luck with your down dwellers, slick. You got this."

Being dead has its perks, too. Who would have guessed I'd ever meet Elvis, or see Amy Winehouse and Freddy Mercury perform? This is by far the best pub I've ever been to. Just as I'm about to order a fresh pint, I see Gabe peeking through the window as if trying to find someone. I wave while beckoning him over. The moment we lock eyes, he freezes. He throws me a stressed look and turns on his heels. Okay, that's it. I'm done with being Mr nice guy. This is the second time he's ghosting me. I leave as quickly as I can, hoping to catch up with him. What if he's closed his eyes, called out his assignment's name and left? I'm in front of the pub, but he's nowhere to be seen. I'm too late. If he keeps avoiding me like this, I'll never figure out what's going on. I'm at my wit's end, but then I see a piece of paper lying in front of the pub's window. It is a handwritten letter. I pick it up and carefully unfold it. It's an instruction letter, for an assignment to look after a down dweller. My own letter is still safely tucked away in my pocket, so this one belongs to someone else. I briefly hesitate reading it.

But then again, how am I supposed to return it to the rightful owner if I don't know whose it is?

Dear Mr Wandsworth,

Oh my goodness, this is Gabe's instruction letter.

Welcome back as a valued member of our team. Your first job concerns a couple living in Reading.

Hey, that's where I grew up. What a coincidence.

This couple was recently bereaved of their only child.

Wow, that's really sad.

They're struggling to get by, now that their son has passed away.

I can imagine.

Mum is constantly watching fifties sitcoms, while Dad is mostly to be found at the homeless shelter cooking residents a full English fry up.

Wait, what? This sounds familiar.

Due to unprocessed grief, this couple stopped communicating, and are now on the brink of losing each other as well. This is what Mr and Mrs Jones need:

Oh no, no, no, no. These are my mum and dad. For goodness' sake, Gabe has been assigned to my parents! This explains a lot. Now I get why Gabe is trying to avoid me at all costs. What is he supposed to say? 'Hey Calum, I'm seeing your parents on a daily basis, cause I'm looking after them. Can't tell you anything though, nor can I let you visit them'? I take a deep breath and continue reading.

- *Grief counselling/support group.*

- *A reminder of why they fell in love.*

- *A shared interest/new passion as a couple.*

Once these requirements are met, your assignment ends. Since you've worked for the Afterlife Agency before, you know the drill. Should you have any questions or concerns, please do not hesitate to get in touch.

Kind regards,

Olga Jensen-Scott
Office Manager
Monday-Eternity
09.00-17.00

I should have known. How could I have missed this? Gabe must have been beside himself. This is a proper conflict of interests. On the top left corner, there's a code consisting of several numbers, letters and symbols. It's the elevator code Gabe's been using to visit my parents. If he's forged a bond with them, he won't be needing it anymore. He can recite their names, and the date he last saw them, to make his way down there in the blink of an eye. I have so many mixed feelings right now. I feel for Gabe, yet I'm upset he didn't tell me. Now that I know my parents have been assigned to by the afterlife agency, I'm worried sick about them. I don't doubt Gabe's competence in looking after them, but I never realised they were having such a hard time. 'Losing a child is the worst thing that could possibly happen to a parent', I overheard my aunt tell Mum, when she visited me in the hospital. All those hours at night when I couldn't sleep, because my pain medication wouldn't kick in, I worried who would be worse off after I was gone, Mum or my dad. My mum has always been a homemaker, taking care of me, Dad, and Daisy, our beagle. Dad has a nine-to-five job working as a financial consultant. At weekends they have dinner parties, or drinks with a circle of close friends they've known since high school. I've never been abroad. Our summer holidays have always been at the same dog friendly hotel at the coast. By the time I was old enough to venture out on my own, I got sick. I don't have any siblings. Growing up, Mum used to say they didn't try for a second one, cause I was everything they'd hoped for. Later on, I found out conceiving me hadn't been easy, which probably led to me being their only kid. I had a blast growing up. Some people might argue that an only child is a lonely child, but as far as I was concerned, that didn't apply to me. When I was six, we got Daisy as a puppy. She and I were best buddies from the beginning, and partners in crime when we'd roam the streets together. Every day after school, she'd wait for me to come home. As I grew older and started hanging out with my friends after school, I'd still take Daisy with me whenever I could.

I miss her wet nose kisses late at night, as she tried snuggling up to me, fully aware she wasn't allowed on my bed. In reality, we slept side by side nearly every night. I wonder if my best bud is still alive. When I got sick, she wasn't exactly a pup anymore. At the hospital they wouldn't let me see her, due to health and safety regulations. In the final stage of my life, I stayed at a hospice. They'd let her come visit me for an hour or so every day. It was the highlight of my day. She would drop her favourite squashy toy on my bed, hoping I'd play catch with her. At that point I could barely sit up anymore, so I'd let Mum or Dad play fetch with her, while I cheered her on from my bed. After I died, my parents lost so much more than just me. I mean, losing me must have been devastating in itself, but they lost a way of life, too. We were a family together, the three of us, and Daisy. We had different things going on that kept us busy during the day, but we always ended up together at some point. On top of that, my parents never missed a match. My dad, otherwise a fairly timid man, would tell anyone willing or unwilling to hear that I was his son. Then he would elaborate on my achievements on and off the field, which weren't that impressive to begin with, but he'd made it sound as if I was one goal short of being the next Messi. It must have felt so empty with me being gone for good. No more Sunday morning fry ups, long walks with Daisy, or going to the chippy after we'd won a game. Conversation would always flow effortlessly between the three of us. Somehow that must have stopped after I passed away. Gabe doesn't strike me as a matchmaker, but I hope with all my heart he can save their marriage. Don't think either one would get over another family break-up.

I take another look at the top left corner, where the code's written. I could easily beam myself up there again and take an elevator back to Mum and Dad. I am sorely tempted, but I do remember Gabe telling me that's against the rules. It really sucks though. I've never been so close to being reunited with my parents, but protocol dictates employees are not allowed to visit former friends and family. I could really use a distraction right now, before I do anything rash. I close my eyes and say *Randell Cavendish, first of November.*

The house is empty and quiet when I enter. Gareth and the girls are probably still at the hospital visiting Grace. I walk up the stairs to Randell's room. I don't want to sneak up on him, so I knock.

"Come in, please."

Randell is sitting at his desk finishing his essay.

"Hey there, looks like you've put in some real effort."

"Yep, I'm nearly finished. Let me just email this to my teacher and then I'm done for the day."

After Randell has clicked on send, he looks up.

"Calum, what's going on? You look terrible."

"Do I look any different from an hour ago?"

"Didn't know a ghost could look this pale, but you rose to the challenge, bro."

"Had a bit of a shock, to be honest."

"Really? What's going on?"

"I found out that a colleague who's been giving me the cold shoulder lately has been assigned to look after my parents."

"What? How did you find out?"

"I found his letter of instruction that goes with the assignment. He's been ghosting me for ages, while we're actually on really good terms."

"I'm sorry to hear that. What are you going to do next? Pop in on your parents to have a look for yourself?"

"It's tempting. The letter provides all the info I need to pay them a visit. Thing is, we're not allowed. Our company's CEO forbids agency employees to get in touch with former friends and family."

"That really sucks. They can't honestly expect you not to want to visit your loved ones."

"That's exactly what they do, and strangely enough, I've made my peace with that. I know my parents are in capable hands, and that Gabe will do anything he can to help them out."

"Gabe?"

"My colleague from the agency. He's worked there for ages. Used to be the office manager, but got demoted. He's on field duty again."

"And somehow he got assigned to your parents. What a coincidence."

"Rumour has it our CEO works in mysterious ways. Still trying to figure out what that means, though."

"You look like you could use some cheering up. I know just the perfect way to do so. Come sit on the bed with me."

Randell has picked up his guitar, strumming the strings lightly.

"Mum got me this guitar when I was nine. At first I didn't really care for it, but when I started taking lessons, my fondness for playing grew by the day. Ever since my mum's accident, I haven't touched it though."

Then he starts playing. The first few songs are pop songs I recognise, so I quietly hum along. Then he moves on to some jazz tunes. It's evident that he's got a decade of experience under his belt. Although he hasn't played for months, his fingers move flawlessly. No one has ever played anything for me before. I'm oddly moved.

"I would have played you some blues as well, but I'm not sure that's the right choice under the circumstances. Don't want you to feel any more sad than you already do."

"I'm much better, thank you Randell. That was amazing. You're really quite talented. Don't worry about the set list. It's my job to look after you, not the other way around."

"Why don't we look after each other from now on?"

He puts his guitar on the bed and turns my way. We're sitting side by side, looking at each other properly for the first time. Randell's hazel eyes have little gold coloured specks in them. His skin is smooth, warm, and feels soft under my touch. His upper lip has the slightest hint of a growing moustache. His three-day stubble suits him really well. I have no idea what he thinks about me. I've been wearing the same outfit ever since I passed. A pair of jeans, my favourite hoodie and a pair of brightly coloured trainers that Mum got me for Christmas last year. I'm so glad they didn't stick me in a suit when they buried me. This might not be much to look at, but at least it's me.

"Penny for your thoughts, Calum?"

"I probably look like a mess compared to you."

"I think you look great. Especially considering you're dead."

"Thanks. I don't exactly know for how long I've been six feet under, but I probably feel cold to the touch."

"Then let me warm you up a bit. See if we can raise that body temperature of yours by a couple degrees."

Randell scoots a little closer my way and wraps his arms around me. It feels so good being held like this. I lay my head on his shoulder and briefly close my eyes. I've never felt so alive since I died. When I open my eyes, Randell has an amused look on his face.

"Did you dose off? Thought you didn't need any sleep."

"Theoretically I don't. It just feels so good to be held by someone."

"Someone?"

"Well actually, you. It feels really nice to be held by you."

"It feels really nice to hold you."

I carefully lean in a bit more, my lips almost brushing his.

"Is it alright if I…?"

I can't finish my sentence, cause Randell's lips are locked on mine. I close my eyes for the second time, and for a moment, everything's perfect. Our kissing starts off slowly and carefully, as if afraid to scare the other person off. I shift a little so I can wrap my arms around him, too. Randell leans back inch by inch, slowly pulling me on top of him. Our kissing intensifies. I am raking my fingers through his curls while he is stroking my back.

"I can feel your heartbeat through your shirt."

"I can't feel yours, but don't worry, mine beats fast enough for the both of us."

"So you're not freaking out?"

"Why would I do that?"

"You're kissing a ghost."

"It's the best kiss I've ever had."

"Same here. Have I warmed up a bit?"

"Can't really tell with that hoodie on."

In one swift motion, I take it off. Randell wraps his arms around me as I move back on top of him.

"How about now?"

"To be absolutely sure, I'd have to take my shirt off, too."

A few second later we're skin on skin, putting our theory to the test.

"Don't know about you, but I feel thoroughly warmed up. At least the upper part of me is." I say.

"Wanna test the other half too?"

Before I can answer, I hear voices coming from downstairs. Gareth, Debs and Grace are back from the hospital. I don't hear their usual cheerful chatter, in fact, they're awfully quiet. Then Gareth calls upstairs.

"Randell, can you come down, please? We need to talk about Mum."

Chapter Nine

The whole family is gathered around the table. I'm standing right behind Randell, feeling his anxiety rolling off him. Maisy looks like she's been crying. Debs is almost as pale as me, and Gareth has dark circles underneath his eyes. Debs gets up from her seat to put the kettle on.

"I think we could all use a cup of tea," she says quietly.

"Dad, Debs, what's going on? Did anything happen at the hospital?"

Gareth sighs deeply before he starts speaking.

"At first, everything seemed fine. There hadn't been any episodes for a while. She looked at ease, and well taken care of as usual. We stayed at her bedside for a while. Maisy told her all about Halloween, didn't you dear?"

"I did. I told her about our costumes, and that she's in the Halloween family picture too. I promised her that next year, when we're going as a family again, she gets to be Elsa."

"I'm sure she's really looking forward to that, Maisy," Debs says. "You know what? It's been a busy day, so why don't you go upstairs and watch cartoons? I'll join you in a bit."

After Maisy has bounced upstairs, Debs resumes talking.

"I don't think she needs to hear this again. She got so upset at the hospital."

"What happened there?" Randell asks, growing more anxious by the second.

"Maise and I were bringing the hospital staff some cupcakes in their break room, while Dad stayed with Mum. When we got back, Dad was in a right state."

"I asked Debs to take Maisy to the cafeteria to have a snack, while I talked to her doctors," Gareth continues. "Turned out she had a heart attack. After running a couple of tests, they told us she needs surgery to prevent this from happening again. Thing is, her body isn't strong enough. She very likely won't make it."

"Wait, so she needs surgery to survive, but if they perform said surgery on her, she'll probably die."

"I'm so sorry, Randell, but it seems that way."

"When do we need to make a decision?"

"The doctor said her life is hanging by a thread. She needs that surgery as soon as possible."

"Then what are we waiting for?"

"It's not that easy, Randell," Debs chimes in. "Her body has been through so much already, surgery will be very tough on her, and most likely she won't pull through."

"If we do nothing, she'll have another heart attack."

"There is a third option," Gareth says. "We can switch off her life support and let her go in peace."

"What? You want to pull the plug on Mum?"

"I don't want to take her off life support, any more than you do, Randell. But I don't want your mum to have another heart attack either. Like Debs just said, her body has been through so much. I'm not sure I want her to suffer through surgery, and risk letting her die in an operating theatre alone."

"So, what do we do now?"

"I told the doctor I would discuss things with you guys first. He said we have to come to a decision sooner rather than later. I already called uncle John and aunt Rose. They're coming to stay with us for a while."

"I think we should let Mum go peacefully, surrounded by her family," Debs says.

"I guess you're right," Randell says.

"Uncle John and aunt Rose will be here tomorrow morning. We'll all go to the hospital together. The doctor promised they'll give us all the time we need to say goodbye."

"How are you holding up Dad?" Randell asks.

"Hanging in there, just like the rest of you. I'm so glad I've got you guys. Wouldn't know what to do without you."

"Same here Dad, these past few months have been hard on all of us. I know we can pull through this, as a family, like Mum would have wanted us to. Let's promise each other that no matter what, we keep sharing our thoughts and feelings on how we're doing. We can't do this alone."

"Well said Debs, when did you get all grown up? You're wise beyond your age."

"I had to be, Dad. I've been trying to keep our family from falling to pieces, ever since Mum's accident."

"I'm so sorry, love, but things are about to change. I've decided to step down as CEO. I'll be spending a lot of time at home."

"But Dad, you love your company," Debs says.

"I love you guys more."

"You've worked so hard to be where you are now," Randell adds.

"Truth is, I should have been here all along, rather than burying myself up to my ears in work. Also, now that we've promised each other to be truthful about how we feel, I haven't been doing great lately. I've joined a support group to help me deal with certain things I've been struggling with."

"I'm glad you reached out for help, Dad. Who knows, maybe Mum's been looking out for us all this time, even though she isn't here physically," Debs says.

"Sure, or maybe someone else entirely," Randell answers, while looking at me sideways.

"Listen, I'm absolutely knackered. Let's order some pizza and turn in early. We've got some difficult times ahead of us," Gareth suggests.

At dinner, everyone is awfully quiet except Maisy, who cheerfully chatters about the cartoons she's just watched. Gareth, Debs and Randell barely touch their pizza. I cannot imagine what they're going through right now. They're mentally preparing to say goodbye to their mum, and in Gareth's case, his wife. Of course, nothing will prepare them for the heartbreak to come. All I can do is try my best to help them come to terms with their loss. I hope I'll be around for a while longer, now that I've accomplished the goals I set myself. First of all, I've been looking after Randell, Debs and Maisy. Secondly, I got them Grace and Gus back, the necessary aid in keeping their house and grounds tidy. Thirdly, I made sure Gareth got in touch with professional help, as a start to help him deal with his gambling problem. I have no idea what the original requirements were to help this family out, cause I never received a letter of assignment. The only letter I have is the one about Philip Brisbane. I was asked to fill in on the mum job temporarily, but then Gabe left as office manager. I think Olga kind of forgot that I wasn't supposed to be on this job in the first place. Now I can't imagine leaving. I've grown fond of all of them.

I've grown fond of Gareth, who's accepted help, and finally realises his family needs him way more than his company. Then there's Maisy, who's always cheerful, and loves helping those around her feel better about themselves. What about Debs, who's been taking on so many responsibilities looking after her loved ones? She almost forgot she's a teenager too. Last but not least, there's Randell. Sweet, kind-hearted, smart Randell, who's been struggling for quite a while now. He must have missed his mum so much, not being able to share what's been going on in his life. Against all odds, I've forged a connection with him I never thought possible. He's the only down dweller who can see me, hear me and, strangely enough, touch me. Am I supposed to leave him at some point, when I'll get my next assignment, or will I'll be able to pop in for a visit now and then? We probably shouldn't have kissed. It makes it all the more complicated, especially for him. I'm dead, but he still has his whole life in front of him. We could never really be together, not in a sense I'd like, or crave, to be honest. After dinner, Randell goes straight to his room. I hesitate to go after him. Maybe he needs some alone time right now. Just as I'm about to quietly knock on his door, Randell appears in the doorway.

"Why are you still out there? Come in."

"I thought you might want some time to yourself, seeing what your dad just told you."

"The only thing that's keeping me from freaking out completely is you being here. Please promise me you won't leave."

"I won't Randell. I'm so sorry about your mum."

"Thanks, I can't believe this time tomorrow it will all be over. I won't have a mum anymore. She'll be gone forever."

As we sit down on the bed, I wrap my arms around him.

"I don't know what to say, Randell. I've never known your mum, but from what I understand, she must be really amazing."

"She was, I mean is. She's always looked after me, Debs and Maisy. Dad was away from home a lot, working round the clock as the head of Cavendish Industries. We'd never see him before tea, and afterwards he would retire to his study straight away. Mum made us feel like we mattered a lot. She'd pick us up from school, and drive us around to friends, sport clubs or wherever we needed to be. At home, she'd always have a treat waiting for us. At night, she'd help us with our homework, and before bedtime, we would all kick back and watch a movie together. Some nights Dad would join us. The five of us would crawl under a blanket on the couch, and watch Little Mermaid, or Frozen for the umpteenth time. Those were the best nights ever."

"I can imagine. It sounds like your mum waited on you guys hand and foot."

"She did have her own life. When we were at school she'd go for a coffee, or have lunch with her friends. She had her own online shop selling hand crafted jewellery. She did pretty well for herself, actually. But she would always put us first. You're right, she did wait on us hand and foot. Wish we hadn't taken that for granted."

"I'm sure she loved taking care of you guys. My mum always said she didn't need a thank you for all the work she did around the house, and for looking after me and my dad. Seeing us happy, clean and well fed was a testament to her doing a great job."

"Still wish I could say a proper thank you to her face."

"Maybe you can do so tomorrow, at the hospital. Who knows, perhaps she'll hear you, or sense your presence."

"You think I should prepare a speech or something? It'll probably be the last time I get to talk to her while she's still alive. I don't even know where to begin, and I've got one night to come up with something loving, meaningful, and unforgettable."

Randell looks as if he's on the verge of a panic attack. He's frantically looking for a pen and some paper. When he doesn't spot any, he opens his laptop. He starts typing for a minute or so, deletes a few sentences, resumes typing, and deletes the whole thing. Then he slams his laptop shut and buries his face in his folded arms. I walk up to him and gently lay my hand on the small of his back.

"Listen, I understand you want to say goodbye properly. Whether you'll write a speech tonight or not, won't make a difference. Maybe you'll find the right words tomorrow, and if by any chance you don't, that's okay, too. Most important thing is, you'll be at her side. I'm sure your mum will feel how loved she is by all of you. I think you should get some rest now. You have some tough times ahead of you."

"Do you really think she knows I love her?"

"Of course she does. If she could see you right now, she'd be moved by the effort you're making, but worried by the state you've gotten yourself into. Let me help you get ready for bed. Where do you keep those Spiderman PJs of yours?"

I find them tossed aside in a corner of his room. I better get him tucked in as soon as possible. He can't have a meltdown before he's said his goodbyes. Best way to avoid that from happening is letting him get some rest. He looks dead on his feet by the rollercoaster of emotions he's been through these past few days. As soon as his PJs are on, I send him to the bathroom to brush his teeth. In the meantime, I fluff his pillows and make the bed. Right, all ready for a good night's sleep. As Randell returns from the bathroom, he grabs his phone.

"What do you think you're doing, young man?" I say, using my most authoritative voice.

"What do you mean? Just watching some feed on TikTok."

"Yeah, I don't think so. It's time to get some shuteye."

"You're kidding me, right?"

"Nope, in you go."

I take the phone from his hands, as I steer him towards the bed.

"You do know you're not actually my mum, right?" Randell says as he looks at me indignantly.

"I know. I would have slapped your ass ages ago if I were. Now, get under the covers."

I tuck him in and make sure he's all snug and comfortable.

"Can I get you anything? Glass of water, an extra blanket?"

"No, I'm fine, thanks. Wouldn't mind some company over here."

"Fine, but don't you get any funny ideas in your head? It's bedtime."

"So we're not picking up where we left off this afternoon?"

"Not tonight, love," I say as I gently kiss his forehead."

"Can you stay with me tonight?"

"I wasn't planning on going anywhere. I'll be here for as long as you need me."

"What if I'll never stop needing you?"

"Then I'll be here forever."

"Promise?"

"Pinky promise."

I scoot over to Randell's side. He puts his head on my chest and closes his eyes. Right before he dozes off, he mumbles, "I can feel your heartbeat."

With all my being, I wish he could.

I must have dozed off, cause when I wake up, sunlight's pouring through the crevices in the curtains. Randell is still fast asleep, quietly snoring next to me. His sleeping face looks innocent and peaceful. Like all of this is just a bad dream he'll wake up from as soon as his mum calls him downstairs for breakfast. Sadly, reality is not a bad dream. It's a nightmare that will irreversibly change his life, and that of his family. I wish I could stop time, just to keep him safe from all the hurt and grief that today will bring. I know I can't. The best I can do is stick around and be there for him when things get tough. I don't know for how long that will be, though. I have no idea when this assignment ends, or whether I can still pop round for a visit when it does. I'd better make inquires at the Afterlife Agency as soon as I can. I'll ask them about my extraordinary connection with Randell, too. With any luck, I'll run into Gabe. I'll tell him I know he's been assigned to my parents, and that I'm okay with that. I turn to Randell, and softly whisper in his ear, "Rise and shine, darling. It's time to get up."

Randell yawns, rolls over, and looks at me, bleary-eyed.

"What time is it? Didn't we just go to sleep?"

"I'm afraid not, love. The whole house will be up soon."

"I don't want to get up. I just want to stay here with you."

"Me too, but that's not possible, I'm afraid. We can hide here all day, but it won't stop life from happening."

"I know. I can't believe this is the day my mum's going to die."

"I'm so sorry Randell. I wish with all my heart I could do anything to stop this."

"Will you be here when we get back from the hospital?"

"Of course, the minute you'll step through that door, I'll wrap my arms around you, and never let go."

"At least I have something to look forward to. So what will you be doing all day?"

"I think I'll head up there for a bit, and pay my agency a little visit. There's still some stuff I need to sort out."

"Be careful, okay? Don't get carried away, or you'll end up doing something you'll regret."

"Like what? Throw a tantrum in the Cheeky Rooster? I'll bet they've seen enough of those around there."

"Cheeky Rooster?"

"It's our afterlife pub."

"Of course it is. What I meant is, you've had some very disturbing news about your parents. Don't get tempted into doing anything you're not supposed to do."

"Like paying them a visit?"

"Yes, for instance."

"I won't. Gabe is one of the most capable employees they have up there. He'll take good care of them."

"Good, I'll be heading downstairs then. See you in a bit?"

"See you very soon, Randell."

I take him in my arms once more, holding on so tight I can hear him gasp for air.

"Easy there, Incredible Hulk, leave some for later."

"I will."

I give him one last kiss. Then I take out my assignment letter, tap it twice, close my eyes, and say 'Afterlife Agency'. Before I can worry about what my sudden and swift departure must have looked like to Randell, I'm back where it all started, at the Afterlife Agency.

Chapter Ten

As I walk up to Olga's desk, I can't help worrying about Randell. I wish I could be with him at the hospital today. I know he has his family there, but still. I want to be a bigger part of his life than just the guy who's there when he gets home. I know that's not possible, since I'm bound to the house and its grounds. I can't help fantasising though, what it'd be like if I could take Randell on a proper date. Like dinner or a movie, or a long moonlit walk on the beach. But even if I don't get all that, it would still be worth seeing him. That's why I have to talk to Olga asap. She isn't at her desk, so I scan the room, hoping to spot her.

"Can I help you, sir?"

A young woman in a pencil skirt and blouse appears at my side.

"Oh hi, I hope so. I was looking for Olga."

"She isn't in, I'm afraid, lots of meetings today."

"Can't I wait till she gets back?"

"Her schedule is fairly packed today. I can let her know you dropped by."

"Uhm no thanks, but thanks anyway. I'll see myself out."

Randell won't be back from the hospital for a while. I could go for a pint in the Cheeky Rooster and try my luck again later.

I'm sure Olga will be back at the office at some point. I close my eyes and within seconds, I find myself peering through the pub's window. It's a bit busier than last time, so I scan the bar for anyone I know. Just as I'm about to head in, I spot Olga. She's sitting at the bar, her back turned to me. She's in deep conversation with Gabe. I can't hear what they're saying, but as far as I can tell, they're not chitchatting about the weather. Good to see the two of them together. I can kill two birds with one stone, so to speak. I squeeze myself through a crowd of boisterous young men dressed as Roman centurions. On second thought, that's probably what they are. As I draw closer, I can hear bits of their conversation. Gabe is looking at his shoes while Olga is trying to make eye contact. Neither of them is aware of me.

"He knows Olga, I'm sure of it."

"So what if he does? He's fully aware of what we're doing up here."

"Don't think I can avoid him for much longer. I feel awful. Why did you give me the job?"

"I didn't, Gabe. You know just as well as me, that decision was made by our CEO."

"Be that as it may, things are not going well. Dad's suffering from depression, and Mum's barely hanging in there."

"Did you get them any help?"

"Been trying, but Dad's stubborn, and Mum won't let any-one else take the reins."

"Well, if you did everything you could, then that's that. You can't spend forever on one assignment, or in this case, two down dwellers."

"For Pete's sake, Olga, we're talking about the boy's parents."

"You shouldn't let your feelings interfere with your work, Gabe."

"Easy for you to say. If things don't look up soon, we'll have the two of them in our waiting room before the end of the week."

Oh no, they're talking about my parents. I knew they weren't in a good place, judging from Gabe's letter. Didn't know that any help he's been trying to get them, hasn't caught on. My death was miserable enough. I don't want them to follow in my footsteps and meet an untimely demise. Can't believe Olga has given up on them. Is that what happens? When a down dweller you've been assigned to isn't getting any better? Just give up, and move on to the next assignment, hoping that one will work out better. I can't believe it. On the one hand, I'm furious, but on the other hand I might have been really naïve. I probably got lucky with the Cavendishes. It wasn't an easy feat, but I got them back on track. What if I had failed? Would Gareth have ruined them all with his gambling addiction? Would Maisy be left to fend for herself, after Debs would have got a meltdown from taking on too many responsibilities? What about Randell? Would he have continued his quest on Grindr, taking immense risks? Just the thought alone makes me feel sick to my stomach. This isn't right. They can't just leave Mum and Dad like this. Olga seems determined though. There's not much Gabe can do either once he's reassigned elsewhere. I'm going to have to make my way down there myself. As soon as I've made up my mind, I slowly retreat. I can't let them see me. If they've got the slightest notion about what I'm about to do, they'll try to stop me. As soon as I'm outside, I close my eyes and head back to the agency. I remember where the elevators are from there. When I first got here, it looked like one big maze, but somehow it makes much more sense now. Gabe's letter is in my back pocket. I take it out and read it once more. I'm well aware of breaking the rules here, but they leave me no choice. I'll go about my business very carefully. They won't even know I'm there. I think I know just what to do. I'll take Mum's phone, text some of her friends explaining what's been going on, and wait for help. I've known my parent's friends for ages, I grew up with most of their kids. If they knew Mum and Dad were hanging by a thread, they'd come to their rescue and stage an intervention. Problem solved, Gabe can move on to his next down dweller, and I'll be back in time to see Randell. I type in the code written in the top left corner. The elevator doors close. There's no turning back now. I'm coming home.

As I step out into the sun, I'm a stone's throw away from the house I've lived in my entire life. It still looks the same from the outside, although the weeds in our front garden have grown a little taller than I'm used to. Also, it looks like the grass hasn't been mowed for quite some time. I take a peek through the living room window, which isn't easy due to a thick layer of dust. Mum has always taken pride in keeping her windows spotlessly clean. With all that's been going on, I can imagine that cleaning and gardening haven't exactly been a top priority. Okay, here we go. I'll just pop in for a minute or so, find Mum's phone, send a few texts, and head back. As I enter the living room, there's no one in sight. That's strange. Usually around this time of day, Mum and Dad are having a cup of tea with some home-made shortbread, discussing the news, or local town gossip. Maybe Dad's away cooking at the homeless shelter, and Mum's visiting a friend. The living room looks tidy enough, although the place could really use some hoovering. For some reason I walk straight upstairs to my old bedroom. The door is ajar, like somebody just walked out. I carefully open the door and gasp. Mum's on my bed. She has my pillow propped up against the wall and is slumped against it. She's holding a picture frame in her hand. I know the photo only too well. It's my year twelve school picture, taken when I was seventeen. I wasn't sick back then; it was about a year before all hell broke loose. I'm smiling at the camera, not a care in the world. As I quietly enter the room, Mum looks up.

"Seems like only yesterday you were still with us."

Wait, what, can she see me? Oh no, this cannot be happening.

"Your Dad and I were so happy when you graduated high school. You were so ready to move on to bigger and better things."

Strangely enough, she's looking at the picture again, completely ignoring me.

"Mum, can you see me?"

"Of course, none of that mattered, cause a year after this picture was taken you got sick."

I walk up to my Mum and squat in front of her.

"Mum, can you see me? I'm right here."

"In the beginning, we still had every hope you'd make a full recovery. You were so young, and full of life, with a bright future ahead of you."

"It's fine, Mum. I'm doing alright."

Mum is still talking to my picture, oblivious to me being three feet away.

"When it became clear you wouldn't get better, only worse, our worlds collapsed. We put on a brave face, but inside we were dying alongside you. We were losing our beautiful, talented, gentle son."

At this point, Mum's crying. She doesn't bother wiping her tears, knowing there'll be plenty more to come. I scoot next to her on the bed. I take her hand in mine and put my head on her shoulder. We stay like this for a while.

"Calum, are you here?"

Her question takes me by surprise. I've already established she can't see or hear me.

"I can feel you in the room with me. You're here, aren't you? You've come home to me. My beautiful baby boy."

Oh no, this wasn't supposed to happen. I have to get out of here. I know I shouldn't be doing this, but I can't resist comforting Mum, one last time. I carefully cup her face in my hands and place a kiss on her forehead.

"Bye Mum, I love you."

I all but run out of the room. Oh my goodness, mission failed. I can't go back in there and look for her phone. I have to proceed with far more caution. If I get too close to either of my parents, they can somehow sense me. Maybe I can look for Dad's phone, it's usually lying around somewhere in his study. As I walk past the bathroom, I hear a quiet sobbing. I suppress the urge to knock first and walk straight through the door. Dad's sitting on the toilet, lid closed. He's looking at a jar of pills in his hands. Oh no, he's not seriously about to…Wait, I know that label. It used to be one of the many meds I was on. This one, according to the label, is to help me have an easy bowel movement. Well, at least these pills aren't lethal, as far as I know. Dad's phone is lying on the bathroom sink. Right, Dad's not in any immediate danger, so let's take care of those texts first. I carefully reach for his phone. Dad seems so preoccupied by his own misery he doesn't look up once. I compose a short message saying that he and his wife haven't been doing well ever since I passed, and they're both at their wits' end. If this isn't a cry for help, I don't know what is. I scroll through Dad's list of contacts and send the message to his closest friends. Right, done. Mission accomplished. I'm sure his phone will be ringing in no time. I'm about to make myself scarce when I notice a weirdly shaped bracelet around my Dad's wrist. As I take a closer look, I realise it's made of elbow macaroni bits. Wait a minute, I remember this. When I was in kindergarten, I made this for him, as a father's day present. He was so pleased with it he wore it non-stop for the entire summer. I'm oddly moved he's wearing it again. When I was young, my mum used to say Dad and I were peas in a pod, and always up to no good. In a sense, she was right. We'd giggle about silly things, build forts out of all the fancy throw pillows, have cake for dinner, and ice cream for dessert. When I got older, our relationship changed. We still loved and appreciated each other, but we stopped hanging out like mates. Seeing my Dad's macaroni bracelet, I've never felt so homesick. Without thinking twice, I take his hand in mine. I carefully stroke his bracelet. Dad has stopped crying.

"I miss you, bud."

"Miss you too, Dad."

I softly kiss the weirdly shaped and brightly painted macaroni pieces. Then I get up and leave.

Once I'm outside, I take out Gabe's letter. I'll head back to the Agency, see if I can have a word with Olga about my assignment, before going back to Randell. I close my eyes, tap the letter twice, and say Afterlife Agency. The first thing I see when I open my eyes is Olga. She looks furious.

"Get in my office, now!"

Oh no, she knows what I've been up to.

"Olga, I can explain everything."

"I'm about to explain some things to you, young man."

As I follow her into the office, she walks past her desk into a small room at the back. It's very sparsely furnished. There's a table and two chairs.

"Sit down."

As I sit down, I'm slightly panicking.

"I take it you know I visited my parents?"

"You're damn right I know. What were you thinking?"

"I found Gabe's assignment letter. At first I wasn't planning on going down there at all."

"But you went there, anyway."

"After I found out you were about to leave my parents to fend for themselves."

"What are you talking about?"

"Earlier today, I went to the office to see you. You weren't in, so I went to the Cheeky Rooster. I saw you there with Gabe, who, by the way, has been avoiding me like the plague. I was hoping I could talk to you both to set things straight. Then I overheard your conversation. Gabe said my parents were barely hanging in there, and that he had failed to get them any help. You basically told him; 'good try, too bad it didn't work out, now please move on to your next assignment'."

"You didn't bother to talk to us about it first?"

"You seemed pretty determined to reassign Gabe some-where else."

"You've only heard part of our conversation, Calum."

"That's all I needed to hear."

"Yes, I was going to reassign Gabe. He was beside himself when he got assigned to your parents. He felt terrible about having to keep that from you. On top of that, he wasn't getting anywhere with them, while they clearly needed help. Howev-er, I never said I was going to let them fend for themselves."

"What do you mean?"

"I was going to take over from Gabe myself. I didn't want to risk another employee failing."

"So, you weren't bailing out on them?"

"I would never do that to any down dweller, let alone your parents."

"I didn't know that. I freaked out after hearing you and Gabe. Especially when he said my parents were due for the waiting room any day now."

"Gabe feared for the worst. That's why he requested an emergency meeting with me."

"I'm so sorry Olga, you're right. I should have gone to you first."

"You have no idea what damage you caused when you interfered."

"What damage? I texted some of my parents' closest friends to let them know they weren't in a good place. As soon as I sent the texts, I left."

"Calum, why do you think it is that our CEO won't let us visit friends, family or loved ones down there?"

"Cause it'd be too hard on us to see the ones we left behind."

"Actually, it's the other way around. It'd be too hard on them."

"Why? They didn't see or hear me."

"From the moment you crossed your parents' threshold, they sensed your presence. You didn't even have to connect with them, like you had to with the Cavendishes. The connection was already there. It was forged, the second you were born, twenty something years ago."

"How is that even possible?"

"Because you're their son, not a stranger like Gabe. We had to send a team over there to do damage control."

"What damage? If anything, I got them the help they needed."

"Calum, your parents have been grieving ever since you passed away. Grief is a process with different stages varying from denial, anger, bargaining, depression, and, last of all, acceptance. These stages do not follow a chronological order. They come and go as they please. By visiting your parents, you've triggered all sorts of emotions and feelings they had already processed, at least to a certain extent. Meaning, in the worst-case scenario, they're back to square one."

"I don't know what to say. How are they doing now?"

"Too early to tell, a specialist team has slightly altered their perception of your little visit, so that they have no recollection of ever having felt your presence at home."

"What if they take comfort in knowing I was there?"

"I hear what you're saying, but aeons of experience have taught us that those who are left behind have a harder time processing the different stages of grief, when their departed loved ones keep dropping by unexpectedly."

"What if I take comfort in seeing them?"

"I'm sorry Calum, but life is for the living. Even though your loved ones can feel your presence, they can't see or hear you. They don't know when, or if you'll come back. We've seen down dwellers wasting away, waiting for a deceased relative, or friend to return."

"That's another thing I wanted to ask you about. As it turns out one of my charges can see and hear me."

"That's impossible."

"It all started on Halloween. Gabe told me to be careful, since it's the one and only night down dwellers, and agency employees are connected stronger than ever. Weirdly enough, only one of my down dwellers noticed me. His siblings and father didn't."

"So he can still see you, even though Halloween was last weekend?"

"Yep. Not only that, he can touch me."

"Excuse me?"

I turn a nice shade of red, cause how am I going to explain what Randell and I have been up to?

"Well, uhm. At one point I accidentally bumped into him, and he felt that."

Olga, looks at me suspiciously, like she knows I am holding back some vital intel.

"You bumped into him? Must have been a surreal experience for both of you."

"I can honestly say it has."

"Listen, I don't know what to tell you, Calum. This sounds way above my paygrade, so I'm going to have to get back to you on this one. As far as I know, this has never occurred before."

A firm knock on the door makes us both look up. The lady in the pencil skirt and blouse whom I talked to earlier, is poking her head around the door.

"Please come in Magda. Calum and I were just about finished."

"I thought as much. That's why I'm interrupting. I've got priority mail from corporate to be read upon receipt."

"Thank you, Magda."

As Magda leaves, Olga looks at the envelope.

"We don't get a lot of these down here. In fact, this is my first one. If you can give me a minute Calum."

Olga opens the envelope and starts reading its contents. Then she reads it again, looks up, and sighs.

"Is everything alright?"

"I'm afraid not."

"What's going on?"

"Corporate got wind of your little field trip. They're not pleased, to say the least."

"How did they find out?"

"Our CEO is omniscient and omnipresent, remember?"

"Can I explain myself to Them?"

"I think it's too late. It says in the letter you're being let go."

"Wait, what? The Cavendish family is at the hospital right now, saying their goodbyes to Grace. I need to be there for them when they get back."

"I'll make sure someone else will cover for you."

"You don't understand. I've forged an extraordinary connection with Randell. He's come to rely on me. I've promised I'd be there the minute he'd be home."

"I've got explicit orders not to let you go back there."

"Do you expect me to just move on to the next down dweller?"

"Actually, you're not being reassigned to anyone new."

"Excuse me?"

"You're to join our re-education programme until further notice."

"Your what?"

"It's where deceased down dwellers go, who haven't been deemed fit, to join the Afterlife Agency."

"But I've already joined the agency."

"In your case it's a disciplinary action, for breaking the rules."

"I just explained why I did that, and I'm sorry. It won't happen again."

"I feel for you Calum, I really do. If it were up to me, I wouldn't send you there. Thing is, it isn't up to me."

"Let me speak to someone from corporate. All I need is one minute to explain myself."

"That's not how things work up here."

"When will I get back?"

"When you're deemed fit to join the agency again."

"Deemed fit by who, corporate? So they're calling all the shots? Too bad for them, I'm not going."

I close my eyes and say *Cavendish residence, second of November*. When I open my eyes, I'm still in Olga's office. "

"Sorry Calum, corporate has rescinded your teleportation powers."

"I'll take an elevator then."

"You won't get far. In a minute, two instructors from our re-education programme will come to collect you. If you're thinking of putting up a fight, don't. You'll only make things worse. They can incapacitate you with just the snap of their fingers."

Then two things happen simultaneously. The door flies open, and two men dressed in the exact same navy blue three-piece suit burst in with Gabe following in their wake.

"Are you Calum Jones?" One of them asks.

I merely nod.

"Calum Jones, you've been relieved of your duties at the afterlife agency. You are about to join our re-education programme, till corporate has decided otherwise."

"Wait, this is insane." Gabe jumps in. Why is he being sent there in the first place?"

"You know just as well as I do, he broke the rules," navy blue suit man replies. "He visited his parents when he shouldn't have."

"Oh please, you blame a kid for wanting to save his parents' life? For all he knew, they were well on their way to one of our waiting rooms."

"Still, he should have known better," other navy blue suit man replies.

"Should he though? From the moment he's arrived, he's been getting a raw deal. First of all, he ends up with the wrong down dwellers on his first assignment ever. Secondly, he decides to stick with them anyway, regardless of how utterly inexperienced he is for such a complex task. Thirdly, he was supposed to be replaced on the Mum Job, so he could take on his original assignment, which is looking after Philip Brisbane. That never happened, by the way."

"He stole your letter of assignment, Gabe."

"He didn't steal anything. I lost that letter yesterday when I bolted from the Cheeky Rooster trying to avoid him. Which brings me to my next point. Calum has only been up here very shortly. As far as I know, I am his only friend and confidant, yet corporate gave me a job, making it impossible for me to have an honest conversation with him."

"He should have talked to his supervisor, Ms Jensen-Scott."

"He tried, but he overheard me telling Olga his parents were barely hanging in there. If anything, I should be sent away, not him."

"We're here to bring in Calum, not you, Gabe. If you have a problem with that, take it up with corporate."

"So, this is it? He's fired without a fair hearing? Even down dwellers go to trial first, before getting sentenced."

"We need to get going Gabe, we have other things planned today."

"Wait, stop," I interject. "I'll go willingly, I promise. I'm the only one here who messed up, and I'll take full responsibility for that. All I'm asking for is a chance to say goodbye to Randell. He'll be heartbroken if he gets home, and I won't be there. He's just lost his mum, and I'm all he has right now."

"Young man, we're not negotiating the terms of a disciplinary action corporate has imposed upon you." One of the navy blue suit men says.

"Take him, it's time," the other navy blue suit man says.

Both men pull me to my feet and steer me out of the office. I can't believe this is happening. I turn around to face Gabe.

"Please tell Randell I'm sorry, and that I…uhm, you know…that I …"

"Hang in there Calum, I'll get you back up here in no time."

Both navy blue suit men snap their fingers simultaneously, and then I'm gone.

Chapter Eleven

When I open my eyes, I'm in what looks like another waiting room. This time, I'm not the only one here. There're eight of us. We're a colourful bunch, as far as I can tell. Two of my fellow waiting room delinquents look around my age, a boy and a girl. The boy is constantly feeling in his pockets, like he just realised his phone's missing. The girl looks bored and keeps twisting a ring around her index finger. Then there are three men and one woman, presumably somewhere in their thirties. They seem to know each other, cause they're talking in hushed voices, occasionally glancing at the door. Last but not least, there's a man in his late twenties, I think. He looks different than the others. He's wearing a three-piece suit that would have looked great on any gentleman a good hundred years ago. On top of that, his whole demeanour is rather aloof and stiff. I suppose the only thing all eight of us have in common is that we have not been deemed fit to join the agency. Just as I'm wondering for how long they'll keep us here, the door opens and another navy blue suit man appears.

"Greetings to all of you. My name is Seth, but you can forget about that straight away, since you won't be seeing me again. Right, I'm just going to call the register, making sure everyone's here who needs to be."

"Calling the register? What is he talking about? We're not in maths class."

Seth seems unperturbed and takes out a sheet of paper.

"Just raise your hand if I call your name. Okay, let's see; Tara Davenport, right, there you are."

The ring twisting girl raises her hand.

"Let's see who's next on my list," Seth continuo. "Paulo Rodriguez? Yes, great, got you."

"The boy who keeps checking his pockets just gave a little wave.

"Ah, the four siblings; Rudy, Cal, Mark and Haley Heslop, I see you over there."

The group of four barely look up as Seth calls out their names.

"Then who do we have here? Right, Calum Jones?"

"Over here," I say.

"Great, thanks, and last but not least, Andrew Wandsworth."

The man in his late twenties looks up and raises his hand. But wait, Andrew Wandsworth? I've heard that name before. Is he? But he can't be. Yet, he has to be. How many Andrew Wandsworths, dressed as a Charles Dickens contemporary, would I run into down here? This has to be Gabe's partner. Before I have time to have a word with him, Seth continues.

"Most of you know why you were sent to our re-education programme. For those who don't, please allow me to refresh your memories. All of you but one are former agency employees gone rogue. Each and every one of you is here for a variety of different reasons. Some of you have bailed out on your assigned down dweller, others have been caught stealing. One of you has caused a bar brawl in the Cheeky Rooster, and two of you have been caught trying to get in touch with family or loved ones, which is strictly against company rules. So, in a minute, you'll be escorted to our pretty impressively equipped classroom. Here you'll be taking a number of courses, all of which will be concluded by an exam. Once you've passed all of your exams, you will be evaluated by corporate. If you pass, you're welcome to join the Afterlife Agency again. If not, there will be consequences. Please follow me."

Oh great, a rare perk of being dead is no more studying for exams or late night homework to finish. Apparently, that's about to change.

We follow Seth into a classroom, in which two rows of tables have been set up. We all get to sit in pairs. Ring girl and pocket boy, team up straight away. The four siblings split up in pairs, and have already chosen their seats. That leaves just me and Andrew. As I walk up to Andrew at the only table left, I ask him if it's okay if I join him. He nods, but barely acknowledges me.

"If I may have your attention, class, my job here is done. I will leave you all in the more than capable hands of Ms Finch. Hopefully we'll never meet again, which means you've passed the course."

With a final wave Seth leaves as a slender woman enters the classroom. To my relief, she's not wearing a navy blue suit. I have seen enough of those for the next millennia. She's in a flower patterned two piece that brings out the hazel brown colour of her eyes.

"Hello class, it's my pleasure to meet you. As you've just heard, my name is Ms Finch. I will be your coach for the duration of this course and help you find your way back to our wonderful Afterlife Agency."

For whatever reason, this woman is giving me the heebie jeebies. In hindsight, those navy blue suit men weren't so bad after all. I can't quite put my finger on it, but her friendly demeanour seems a bit too perky. The rest of my Shawshank classmates don't seem bothered in the least. Most are quietly chatting among themselves, or just looking bored as well, hell. Ms Finch is handing out a pile of worksheets.

"Let's get started everyone. We've got a lot of ground to cover today. Don't worry, there will be breaks in between lessons. As a special treat, I made you all some sweet tea and carrot cake. Who says school isn't cool?"

You've got to be joking me. I've had some awkward teachers back in my days, but this is cringe on a whole new level. Who does she think we are? A bunch of primary school pupils eager to show off to her? I look around me to see if anyone else feels the same way, but again, no one seems bothered. Our first lesson starts with a presentation about the Afterlife Agency. Truth be told, it would have been useful if they had shown me this upon arrival. After the presentation, Ms Finch dives straight into the ethical workings of the company. There is very little interaction between us and her. Once she's finished her lecture, we're asked to fill in a number of worksheets. Most questions relate to what she's just told us, so it's not hard. Yet Andrew and I are the only one doing any work. Ring girl and pocket boy are doodling on their worksheets, and the four siblings are ignoring them altogether. After half an hour, Ms Finch announces a break.

"Listen up everyone. The first part of today's class is over. You can all enjoy your break now. If you exit through that door, you'll find our students' outdoor break area. There is sweet tea and carrot cake on the picnic table. Please leave your worksheets on the table. I'll be having a little look at them."

The four siblings are the first ones out the door. Pocket boy and ring girl soon follow. Andrew dawdles, as if he's dreading to go out there. He fiddles with his pocket watch for a minute, gets up and walks out. As I step into our break area, the sunlight takes me by surprise. I'm in a spacious garden with several picnic benches connected by gravelled paths. There are a couple of lounge chairs on a neatly mown patch of grass. Planters, hanging baskets, and tubs are filled to the brim with all sorts of colourful flowers and plants. One thing is missing, though. It takes a minute before I realise there aren't any insects. With a garden this size, and such a diversity of flowers and plants, you would expect to hear bees humming, wasps buzzing, and grasshoppers chirping. None of that applies here. The only sounds I hear are from my classmates chattering. I spot Andrew on one of the picnic benches. He looks lonely and forlorn. I pour two cups of sweet tea and walk up to him.

"Hi, I thought perhaps you'd fancy a cup of tea."

"Oh right, thank you."

"Do you mind if I sit here?"

"Suppose not, go ahead."

"Thanks, so what are you in for?"

"Why do you want to know?"

"Guess I'm just making conversation. I'm in for reaching out to my loved ones, my mum and dad, to be exact. You don't seem like the kind of guy who's in here for theft or causing a brawl in the Cheeky Rooster."

"I've never been to the Cheeky Rooster."

"So you're the only one who isn't a former Afterlife Agency employee?"

"True, I've never been up there."

"Then what got you down here?"

"It's a long and complicated story."

"I don't know how long our break lasts, but I'm listening."

"Very well, as I've just told you, I never made it to the Afterlife Agency after my death."

"May I ask why?"

"I sort of took my own life."

"Sort of?"

"I didn't mean to, but I wasn't being careful either. I lost someone I loved dearly during the first world war. After that, I just more or less gave up on myself. Nothing seemed worth doing anymore. I started drinking, neglected my duties in parliament, and ruined my reputation. About a decade after the war had ended, I went for a swim at night time. Shouldn't have drunk that much wine prior to my little dip in the lake. I don't remember exactly what happened, but somehow I got into trouble, and drowned."

"I'm so sorry to hear that. What happened next?"

"I woke up in a waiting room. After a while, a woman walked in and said I had entered the afterlife. She told me since I had quite some unresolved issues, I couldn't be employed at the Afterlife Agency."

"So, where did she take you?"

"A factory."

"Sorry?"

"I was put to work sowing navy blue three-piece suits for hours on end, alongside other men and women. Once our shift ended, we were told to sit in the break room till our next one. We had this huge screen up there playing promotional videos made by the afterlife agency, telling us that as soon as we'd dealt with our unresolved issues, we'd be employed there."

"How are you supposed to deal with your issues, if you're sowing suits all day long?"

"After every shift they had these counsellors come in, inviting us to talk to them about our lives, before we passed. For a long time, I didn't accept the invitation. Why on earth would I want to share my feelings with a complete stranger who would never understand anything I've been through?"

"So how did you end up here, then?"

"After a while, the monotony of every day being the same got to me. So one night I did decide to talk to someone. Once I started talking, I couldn't stop. It was like I bottled up years of grief, pain, and anger. Once I uncorked it, there was no stopping any of it from pouring out."

"So basically you started therapy."

"That's what they call it these days, yes. Back when I lived, we didn't have that sort of thing. Especially not for the kind of issues I was dealing with. But it helped to get things off my chest. I started to feel better and somehow lighter each day."

"I'm glad you got the help you needed. So what happened next?"

"One day I was asked to drop by at our supervisor's office. He said I'd been working hard for quite some time now, never causing any trouble. He added that he had received word from my counsellor about my personal progress. He told me I was ready to join the Afterlife Agency."

"Wow, that must have been great."

"It was, but not for long."

"Why is that?"

"First thing I did after receiving the good news was ask him about my loved one. I wanted to know if he was up there as well."

"What did he say?"

"He told me I was going to be assigned somewhere else entirely, so I wouldn't bump into him."

"What?!"

"Corporate thought he'd be too much of a distraction, and would disrupt my healing process."

"That's absurd. If anything, it would have been the cherry on top of all your hard work. You'd finally be reunited with the one you lost so cruelly."

"That's what I thought. I tried to reason with them, but they wouldn't budge. I shouted at them, cried, pleaded, but nothing helped. So one night I broke into my supervisor's office and searched through his file cabinet for any information that could help me get in touch with the love of my life. Just as I stumbled upon the file I was looking for, I got caught."

"And you were back to square one in your rehabilitation process."

"Sort of. That's how I ended up here. Think corporate did feel a bit bad for me, so they signed me up for this course. If I pass, they'll let me join the agency, anyway."

"So, what are you planning on doing now?"

"Keep my head down, pass the course, and work for the agency. Everything's better than being stuck here, especially with these imbeciles."

"Right, I take it you mean the rest of the class?"

"Except you. You seem like a bright enough chap."

"Thanks, I guess."

"Once I'm up there, I hope to gather more intel. Maybe someone has heard of him."

"Actually, I have."

"Sorry?"

"I've heard of him."

"I've never mentioned his name. How do you know who he is?"

"Cause he mentioned you. You're talking about Gabe, aren't you?"

"You've met him?"

"After I passed, Olga picked me up from the waiting room. She brought me straight to the Afterlife Agency to receive my first assignment. Gabe was the office manager at the time."

"How do you know we're talking about the same person?"

"After a rocky start, I got to know him a bit. Over pints at the Cheeky Rooster he told me about his life. How the two of you met, fell in love, and tried to have a life together, which couldn't have been easy in your time."

"It wasn't, especially since I was in politics. My father was Lord Wandsworth. My feelings for Gabe would have ruined both our careers and reputation. But we were in love, and we longed so much for a life we knew we could never have. Luckily my family had this little cottage in the countryside where we could love each other freely to an extend I never thought possible. As time passed, we became more reckless. One night I went home with Gabe, something I should have never done. One of his staff alerted Gabe's father, who walked in on us the next morning. Needless to say things didn't end well. Gabe was shipped off to war. I begged him not to go, but he said it would only be temporary. He'd make his way back to me as soon as he could. Sadly, he made his way home in a coffin."

"I'm so sorry, Andrew, for both of you. It must have been so hard having to keep your relationship on the downlow."

"After all this time, I'm not even sure if he still loves me. So much has happened, and so much time has passed."

Before I can respond, Ms Finch appears, smiling broadly.

"Hello everyone, I hope you've enjoyed your refreshments. I'm afraid our break has come to an end. Let's resume today's class, shall we?"

We all follow her inside. Our worksheets are neatly stacked on her desk. Each of our desks has a reader and a fresh pile of worksheets on it.

"Well, class, we've worked hard earlier, but like I said before. We've got quite a lot of ground to cover. In front of you, you'll find a reader titled 'History of the Afterlife Agency, and its impact on mankind'. Please start reading the first three chapters and complete the worksheets. Speaking of which, I've corrected the ones you've filled in earlier today. Some of you have done a great job, for others there is definitely room for improvement. Please bear in mind that whether you'll pass the course or not, will depend on everything you'll do in here."

We quietly set to work, at least Andrew and I do. The four siblings are folding paper planes out of their worksheets. Pocket boy is staring apathetically in front of him, while ring girl is blowing spit bubbles. After about fifteen minutes, Ms Finch looks up.

"Calum, might I have a word with you, please?"

"Uhm, okay, after class?"

"Let's step into the storage cupboard for a minute, please."

I follow Ms Finch, wondering what in the afterlife could be so important that we need to converse in a freakin storage cupboard.

"I know this is quite unconventional, so bear with me, please. First of all, I want to congratulate you on the work you've done so far."

"Thank you, Ms Finch, but this couldn't wait?"

"Well, it's not just that Calum. I've read your file, and the reason you've joined our re-education programme."

"So?"

"You claim to have made a connection with one of your down dwellers in a most extraordinary way."

"That's because it's true."

"So he can see and hear you?"

"And touch me."

"Touch you? Why would he want to do that?"

"Why indeed?"

"Thing is Calum, have you talked to corporate about this?"

"I tried, but they wouldn't listen. All those navy blue suits cared about is getting me shipped off to this re-education programme as quick as their penny loafers could carry them."

"They can be quite insensitive, I agree. That's why I want you to know that I do care. As it happens, I'm not the only one. Seth cares too."

"Well, thanks for your sympathy, Ms Finch. Will that be all?"

"Not exactly, uhm Seth and I are running a programme to test the limits agency employees are capable of."

"Don't think corporate would be down with that."

"Corporate doesn't need to know about our little side track. We've been trying to get them to listen to us for ages. Now it's time to put some of our theories to the test, and gather evidence. Once that's done and taken care of, we'll take our findings straight to our CEO."

"Hoping to get a promotion out of it?"

"Of course not. Our intentions are completely altruistic. However, we'd be more than willing to become our CEO's right hand in pursuing more knowledge."

"So, what do you suggest? I go back down there, and test my so-called abilities on another down dweller?"

"I'm afraid that's not possible, but we could sneak your special down dweller up here?"

"Anyone who comes up here has passed. The down dweller I connected with is alive and kicking."

"For now, he is. I'd love to have a look at the neuropaths in his brain when he connects with you."

"What are you talking about? You can't kill an innocent down dweller just to prove one of your theories. Are you mad?"

"It's in the name of science."

"It'll be cold-blooded murder. I'm devastated I'll never see Randell again, but I'll be damned if I let you, or anyone else, hurt him."

"Why do you care? He's just a down dweller you were assigned to."

"No, he wasn't. He was, no, he is, the sweetest, smartest, most beautiful soul I've ever met."

"Good, your teenage infatuation makes your bond all the stronger. Can't wait to run some tests up here."

"If you'll do that, his family will suffer another huge loss. Randell's mum just died. All they have left is each other."

"I really feel for them Calum, I do. But you have to try and see things in perspective. There are eight billion down dwellers below. One more or less doesn't make a difference."

"It makes all the difference to me."

"Even if you get to see him again? Didn't you just say how much you miss him?"

"I do, but I'd rather be miserable and lonely without him than cutting his life short and taking him away from his loved ones. Cause I know what that feels like, and let me tell you, it's horrible."

"I'm sorry you feel that way Calum, but we don't need your consent for this."

"I'm telling corporate, Olga, Gabe, everyone. Hell, I'll pay our CEO a little visit myself if I have to."

"Don't be ridiculous dear, who would believe you? Besides, you'll never get that far. With the snap of my fingers, I can send you anyplace I want."

"Really? Hard to imagine being anywhere worse than this rank smelling storage cupboard."

"You think you hit rock bottom, dear? What do you think happens to any of your classmates who don't pass this course? I'm betting on the four siblings, and that boy and girl who sit up front."

"What do you mean?"

"Well, they don't get to re-join the agency, and I'm not taking them back in my class, I can tell you that much."

"Where will you send them?'

"Our re-education programme has different circles, so to speak. Right now, you're in one of the top ones, meaning if you pass this course, you get to be an afterlife employee again. For those who refuse to live up to our high, but fair standards, there are more bespoke circles."

"Bespoke?"

"Let's put it like this. If you behave like garbage, you shall be surrounded by it. All day, every day, until it feels like eternity, which it probably is. So here's your choice: you either co-operate, or I'll make sure you'll end up in the worst place imaginable. Oh, and we'll take Randell, anyway."

This cannot be happening. I knew something was off with Ms Finch, but this surpasses my worst nightmares. I don't care where I'll end up, but in each and every scenario, Randell dies.

All because I forged a connection with him. No one up here has ever seen. I have to try to buy myself, and most of all Randell, more time.

"Okay, you win. I'll fully cooperate. On one condition. I want to finish this course. I was sent here for a reason, and I want to prove to Olga, Gabe and our CEO that I'm worthy of joining the agency again."

"Fine, this course will last another day. Guess I can give you that much. Now that we've settled our business, why don't you join the rest of your class?"

"Yes, ma'am."

"Oh and Calum, I knew I could count on you, my dear. Great to have you on board."

I look at my feet, cause if I see one more smug smile, I'll lose it. I walk back to my desk in a daze. Andrew looks up, noticing my distress.

"Calum, what's going on? You've been gone for ages. What did you two talk about?"

"Can't talk right now, wait till after class."

Andrew nods, and goes back to work, looking sideways every so often. I don't get any work done, cause I can't focus for more than two seconds without feeling sick to my stomach worrying about Randell. Tomorrow I'll be a test subject alongside the love of my afterlife. And all of it will be my fault.

Chapter Twelve

After class has finished I practically flee into our break area. I sink down on one of the picnic benches, head resting on my arms.

"What has got you all up in a mood, Calum? Anything happened in that closet?"

"Can't believe I'm saying this, but I wish I never came out of that one."

"Did Ms Finch say anything to you?"

"She said plenty. For instance, how she wants to run tests on me, and on one of the down dwellers I was assigned to."

"Why on earth would she want to do that?"

"She got wind of an extraordinary connection I forged with one of them. Now she wants to dissect his brains to figure out what makes our bond so special."

"That's awful, you should report her."

"I can't. Apparently, she can whisk me away with just a snap of her finger to any place she likes. And I don't mean a good one."

"So, what are you going to do now?"

"I'm trying to buy me and Randell some time. This course will last another mind-numbing day, which, under normal circumstances, I would dread. Once this course is finished she'll bring Randell up here, and use both of us as lab rats."

"Doesn't give you much time to come up with an escape plan."

"I know, so I'm open to suggestions, if you have any."

"I'll think about it, and get back to you, as soon as I've come up with anything."

"Thanks, really appreciate it. Don't want you to get into any trouble, though. You're so close to joining the agency."

"Not sure that I want to anymore, after all I've seen and heard."

"The afterlife is far from perfect, but that doesn't mean it's not worth experiencing."

"Any life up here or down below feels bleak at best without Gabe."

"Just so you know, I think he feels the same way."

"What do you mean?"

"When Gabe was office manager at the Afterlife Agency, every assignment letter was signed by him personally."

"So?"

"He always signed off with Gabe Wandsworth."

"He never forgot about me."

"Even more so, he kept you as close as he could by taking your name."

"We used to joke about this, back when we were alive. How we would call ourselves if marriage was an option. Gabe insisted on being called Wandsworth when no one was around. It was the best feeling ever. I don't think I'll ever get to call him by my name again."

"Don't be too sure about that. In my time, people say, it ain't over, till it's over."

"You're right. After I lost Gabe, I made the mistake of giving up on everything else in life, including myself. I won't let that happen again. We'll figure a way out of it."

"Good to see you've found your 'can do' attitude."

"I hope you don't mind me asking Calum, but you look rather young. Did you die in combat as well?"

"Nope, the only thing I tried to fight was my illness. I got sick and didn't make it."

"Sorry to hear that. Is that why you visited your parents? You must have missed them terribly."

"I did, but that was not the reason. Gabe was assigned to look after them. I overheard a conversation between him and Olga, from which I took that they were barely hanging in there. I got really worried, so I decided to have a look for myself."

"I thought you said Gabe was the office manager?"

"He was, but then he got demoted. Olga took over from him."

"How curious. I've always known Gabe to give it his all in everything he does."

"True. He worked so hard, rarely taking any breaks."

"So how did you end up bonding with a down dweller to such an extend Ms Finch wants to conduct experiments?"

"Truth be told, I'm not sure. I wasn't even supposed to get the mum job. I was assigned to someone else, but somehow I ended up at the Cavendish residence. The agency asked me to fill in temporarily, but soon I had bonded with everyone in the family. They said I simply had to see my assignment through."

"That's odd. So you forged a connection with all of them, yet only one can see and hear you?"

"It started the morning of Halloween. I was keeping an eye on Randell, since he had been struggling for a while. When he woke up, it was complete mayhem at first. Neither of us expected a full encounter."

"So what happened next?"

"I tried to keep my distance for a while, and give Randell some space. That went sideways, though. We got into a fight and he left. I was beside myself, cause I'm bound to his house, and couldn't follow him. When he got back, he wasn't in a very good place. I tried to comfort him as best as I could. From that moment on, we kind of bonded real strong. Not long after, we could even touch each other."

"Touch each other? All in all three powerful senses; sight, sound, and touch. Was there any need to touch your down dweller?"

"Ahem, no, there wasn't. Other than that, we both wanted to."

"I see."

"Really? Cause I don't."

"For someone so smart you can be really thick, Calum. Your connection is extraordinary, because you fell in love, and from where I can see, so did he."

"That's insane. We barely know each other. I admit we kissed, and cuddled, and I slept next to him, but that was for professional purposes only. He couldn't be left on his own at the time."

"You remind me of Gabe and I, when we started courting. He might have told you we met at boarding school when we were still very young. We took a liking to each other quite fast. Needless to say we became best friends, and near inseparable. When we got older, we knew there was more than just friendship. Both of us were too afraid to act upon it, though. Not just because it wasn't accepted back in those days, but we didn't want to risk our friendship either. After we left boarding school, we both went to Oxford. Gabe pursued a career in medicine, and I pursued one in law. Right before exams, we often had study session together, cramming as much knowledge as we could, in a mere few nights. After a particularly long session, we had a little nightcap to unwind. One thing led to another, and we finally admitted to each other how we felt. We spent the night together. It was the best one of my life. After that, we kept seeing each other romantically, yet were always afraid someone would find out."

"Randell and I never got to that point. Getting to tell each other how we feel. It wouldn't have mattered anyway. I'm dead, and he's alive. It would have never worked out."

"That's what people used to think about me and Gabe. Back in my days, two men courting was seen as unnatural, unhealthy, and most importantly unholy. We proved them wrong. Being with Gabe felt as natural as breathing. It was the happiest time of our lives, and being intimate together felt sacred to us. What I'm trying to say is, don't let society define your feelings or your relationship. As long as there's a chance of love, go for it. Regardless of however brief it may be."

"Thanks for sharing, Andrew. I suppose you're right, but by this time tomorrow, I'm not sure if I still have a shot. Especially if our brains are being dissected in the name of science."

Before Andrew can answer me, the sound of a horn pierces the relative silence of our break area. Moments later, Ms Finch appears.

"Morning everyone. I am glad to see you all well rested, and good to go for another day of education."

"Wait what? It's morning already? I know time works differently up here, especially when you don't need sleep or any sustenance, but still. Andrew and I have been talking for quite some time now, which I don't regret. It's just that neither of us has come up with a plan to get us out of this mess. Ms Finch seems oblivious to my obvious discomfort and continues.

"If you pass today's exams, and have fulfilled all requirements concerning this course, you are very likely to re-join the agency. So today is a cause for celebration, if you play your cards right. So please, all of you, put your best foot forward."

I know exactly where I want to put my foot, but I can't say that out loud. I follow Ms Finch back inside. Our day starts with a recap of what we did yesterday. Then we get to watch another video on how to effectively help out a down dweller. Afterwards we're handed a case study, which we have to discuss in pairs. Ms Finch walks around the classroom taking notes. Thank goodness Andrew is in a talkative mood, cause I can barely get a word out. I'm worried sick about what they'll do to Randell.

"Listen up everyone, we're halfway through our final day at this re-education programme. After the break, there will be several exams on topics discussed during this course, namely; the inner workings of the afterlife agency and its history. There'll be an exam on rules, regulations and ethical dilemmas, and last but not least, how to effectively help out your down dweller. Once the exams are finished, you can wait in the break area for your results to come in."

Great, we have a very short window of opportunity to come up with a grand escape.

I silently pray with all my heart Andrew's come up with something, cause my brain feels like it's filled to the brim with cotton candy. As soon as we've taken a seat on one of the picnic benches, I look pleadingly into his eyes.

"I've got nothing, Andrew, absolutely nothing. Please tell me you've got our upcoming prison break figured out. After the exams we're done for. At least I'll be."

"Calm down, old chap, or you'll get yourself into a right state."

"Think I'm already there, Andrew."

"My father used to say; if you find yourself in a pickle, take a step back, and remain calm at all times."

"Wonderfully said, has he ever mentioned anything about how to bust out of an afterlife re-education programme?"

"He hasn't, but that doesn't mean it's impossible. Is there any way we can warn Randell?"

"I can't blink my way down there anymore. Corporate has revoked my teleportation privileges. The only way I can think of is by elevator. I do remember the code I used to get there. Problem is, how do I make my way to an elevator unnoticed?"

"Write down the code for me, will you? Should you fail, I could give it a try. Only thing I can come up with now is to create a diversion somehow. If Ms Finch is distracted, you might be able to make a run for it."

"To where? This place is a maze. I have no idea how to get up there again."

"You're right. Well, that leaves me with only one idea. It isn't perfect, though."

"I'll take anything at this time."

"So here it is. I'll pass my exams and get to join the afterlife agency. As soon as I'm up there, I'll warn someone. If I can't get to Gabe, I'll talk to Olga. She's the manager now, isn't she?"

"She is, but I fear they'll take Randell up here before you can call for help."

"I know it's not ideal, but with a bit of luck, we can catch Seth and Ms Finch in the act."

"What act? The act of experimenting on me and Randell? The act of poking our brains? Even though we're dead, it'll still be excruciating. I told you Randell and I can feel whenever we're around each other."

"I said, it's not ideal."

Before I can reply, Ms Finch appears, looking particularly chipper.

"Right, everyone, the hour of truth is upon us. It's exam time."

As we follow Ms Finch back inside, my legs feel heavier with every step I take. The best plan we've come up with so far is Andrew passing his exams and trying to sound the alarm up there. Only thing is, it'll be too late for Randell. Once he's up here, it's game over. He'll be dead, just like me. I take my usual seat next to Andrew. Our exams are neatly stacked on our desks. As we sit down, Ms Finch sets a timer on a small clock on her desk.

"You have one hour to finish the first exam. Once you're done, you may proceed with the next one, until all three are completed. Please remain seated in silence until the very end, which will be in exactly three hours from now. I wish you the best of luck."

I swear she gives me the tiniest of winks. I open my first exam, all questions are multiple choice. I try to read the first one, but the words seem to dance in front of my eyes. Not that it matters. I'm not going to make it up there, anyway. Not with what Seth and Ms Finch have in mind for me. I randomly circle answers, so I'm done within ten minutes. As I look up, Ms Finch is nodding at me encouragingly, as if saying 'good job, almost there'. We both know I'm winging it big time, but I don't care anymore. My second exam consists mainly of open questions. I take my time with this one, cause the longer she needs to correct them, the more time I'll be able to buy Randell. The third exam is an essay question. It says:

Mr and Mrs X just lost their only child to a terminal illness, at the unfortunate age of twenty-one. Mum's depressed, and Dad doesn't talk about his feelings. Their marriage is hanging by a thread, and they're having a hard time getting their lives back on track. What would your priorities be as their assigned help, and why? Make sure you don't violate any agency rules, and please bear in mind our high standard code of ethics.

They have got to take the absolute piss here. That essay question is about me, and my parents. This can't be a coincidence. I have a good mind of crumpling the exam into a thick wad, and chuck it at Ms Finch's head. That would mean the end of the road for me, and let's face it, for Randell too. Fine, if she wants an essay, she can bloody well have one. I pick up my pen and start writing. I write about the start of my afterlife. What if felt like to suddenly appear in the most depressing, and dull waiting room ever, after having been sick for such a long time. Then I write about my first assignment, what it was like to walk into the afterlife agency, and being employed straight away without so much as an introduction. I jot down that I ended up with the wrong family, but strangely enough, bonded with them, anyway. Especially with Randell, their nineteen-year-old son. I write about how I managed to improve life for all of them, against all odds. I continue writing about how things took a turn for the worse, when I found out my parents weren't doing well, and I feared for their lives. How I stepped in, tried to make a difference, but got found out, and ended up here. Then I add a little side note about ethics and my experience with Seth and Ms Finch. I don't think I'll get full marks on this exam, or any marks at all, for that matter, but I don't care. It feels good to write about my grievances, even though it won't make a difference. As I put down my pen, the alarm clock on Ms Finch's desk starts ringing. This is it, we're done.

"All right everyone, pens down please, time's up, I'm afraid.

I look around me and see that everyone's stopped writing. Ms Finch gets up from behind her desk.

"Since I need some time to correct your work, feel free to venture out into the break area. As soon as I'm done, I'll share the results with you."

I get up, but Andrew remains seated. He looks at my work, then gives me the side-eye. Okay, don't know what that means. Maybe he's come up with a plan. Better head to the nearest picnic bench to discuss it. Andrew finally gets up, but very clumsily. He bumps into my desk, sending my exams flying across the room.

"So sorry, old chap, let me get those for you."

Andrew quickly recovers all my paperwork and stacks it neatly on my desk. Then we head outside.

"What was that all about? Why were you glaring at me? Have you come up with something?"

"Uhm no, I was just looking at you to see how you were doing."

"Well, I'm obviously not great."

"Don't give up hope, okay? No matter what."

"I'll try."

Just as I'm about to discuss any alternative plans of action, Ms Finch walks in. This can't be happening, not this soon. We've barely been outside for ten minutes.

"I'm done evaluating your course work. In some cases it wasn't that much work to be honest. Please follow me inside."

We quietly follow Ms Finch inside as we take our seats one last time.

"Right, let's have a look. First of all we have Ms Davenport. Your work really stood out, in the sense that you didn't get anything done. I'm afraid the agency isn't a good fit for you. Better luck next time, my dear."

Ms Finch snaps her fingers, and ring girl is gone. Everyone gasps, but Ms Finch continues undisturbed.

"Who do we have next? Right, Mr Rodriguez. You did fill in a few worksheets and part of your exams. Truth be told, most of it was gibberish. I think you'll be better suited elsewhere, love."

With another snap of her fingers, pocket boy has left too.

"Ah, who do we have here? It's the Heslop family, Rudy, Cal, Mark and Haley. Regrettably, none of you have qualified to re-join the agency, I'm afraid. So off you go."

Another snap of her finger sends the four siblings straight to goodness knows where.

"Now I finally get to deliver some good news. Mr Wandsworth, you did well both on you coursework, as your exams. So, I am pleased to inform you that you get to join the afterlife agency. Good luck with all of your future assignments."

Andrew looks at me and mouths 'hang in there'. Then he's gone, with just a snap of her fingers.

"So, Mr Jones. That leaves just you and me here. Have you thought about my proposal?"

"Does it matter what I think? You've already made up your mind about bringing Randell up here and run tests on both of us."

"That's true, but it would be so much easier if you were to cooperate."

"Didn't you mention earlier you want to find out why I forged such an extraordinary connection with Randell?"

"Yes, I do."

"You don't have to turn us into lab rats to figure that out. I've been doing some soul searching myself, and truth is, I already know the answer."

"That's great, my dear. Care to share?"

"Randell and I started having feelings for each other. I think we're in love. That's why he is the only down dweller who can see, hear, and touch me."

"That's a lovely hypothesis, dear, but to make sure you've got the right end of the stick, we'll still be conducting those experiments."

"When will Randell be up here?"

"Seth is about to go down there any minute now. We just have to make sure we can travel undetected."

"So, there's no chance of me re-joining the afterlife agency?"

"Love, I've looked at your coursework. You made quite a promising start, however, only half of your worksheets are completed. And as far as your exams go, the last one is missing."

The last one is missing? I'm pretty sure I did a thorough job on that essay question. Weird, it must have got lost in that pile of worksheets and exams on her desk. I shrug my shoulders in compliance with her verdict. It's not like I can appeal to a board about any decisions made here. I just hope that Andrew got up there alright. Even if corporate is keeping him from seeing Gabe, he might get a message across to Olga. It will probably be too late for Randell, and me, though.

"Ah, I just got word from Seth," Ms Finch interrupts my musings. "He's ready, and set to pay Randell a little visit. You will very shortly be reunited with the love of your afterlife."

"How is he going to take Randell's life?"

"Don't worry, it won't hurt. If his calculations are correct, he'll get there by night time. It will be swift and painless."

I sink to the floor in utter despair. This is what hell must be like, waiting for your loved one to get dragged to a place of misery, knowing you're to blame for it. There is not a damned thing I can do about it. I don't know for how long I've been on that floor, but suddenly I hear footstep coming my way. Voices are growing louder by the second. It's done. They've killed Randell.

Chapter Thirteen

It's not Randell or Seth bursting through the door. To my astonishment, it's Gabe and J-dog. They're both out of breath and look rather dishevelled. Ms Finch is as surprised as I am, cause she stares at them open-mouthed. Out of the two of us, she's the first one to regain her composure.

"Might I ask what you are doing down here? You're bursting in on a teacher-student conference."

Gabe looks furious and crouches down next to me on the floor.

"Calum, are you alright?"

"Been better, to be honest."

"Don't worry, we're here now. We won't let her hurt you."

"That's a relief. How did you get up here?"

Ms Finch is looking slightly paler than usual, but she is not one to back down.

"Question is, *why* are you up here? Doesn't the Cheeky Rooster need bartending J-dog? How about you, Gabe? Aren't you supposed to help out some poor down dweller?"

"Right now I'm helping out a friend, whom I should have never left to fend for himself. I'm so sorry Calum."

"What are you talking about? This isn't your fault."

"It is, though. I should have known Olga was in on this all along."

"Sorry, what?"

"Never mind. For now, we have to make sure Randell is safe."

"Think it's too late for that. This navy blue suit guy called Seth is on his way down there to take his life and bring him up here."

"I'd like to see him try. Andrew is keeping watch over him."

"Andrew? You guys met? Gabe, that's great!"

"Our reunion was happy indeed, but brief. We had to act fast to try and save, well, everyone involved."

"So what's J-dog doing here?"

"He made sure that essay you wrote made its way to our CEO."

"My essay? How did it get up there in the first place?"

"I'll explain later. I have to make sure Ms Finch isn't going anywhere."

"Well, gentlemen," Ms Finch replies. "I can't say it's been a pleasure seeing you again, but I have to go now."

With a snap of her finger, she's gone. Except she isn't. She's right there in front of us.

"Oh Ms Finch," Gabe says. "I'd like to inform you that your teleportation privileges have been revoked until further notice."

Ms Finch has turned a shade of grey that isn't particularly enticing.

"You did what? How dare you?"

"Gabe didn't do anything Ms Finch," J-dog jumps in. "Our CEO did."

He walks up to Ms Finch, snaps his fingers, and she's gone.

"How did you do that? Where did she go?" I ask J-dog.

"You think she's the only one around here with finger snap privileges, Calum? I sent her to a place where she can't do any harm."

A firm knock startles all of us. Then Andrew pokes his head around the door.

"Hope, this isn't a bad time, but I just wanted to let you know we've apprehended Seth. He's currently in custody with Ms Finch and Olga."

I don't know why, but I'm so relieved to see his face. I run towards him, and without thinking twice, throw my arms around him.

"Andrew, you made it! I thought I'd never see you again."

"Steady on, old chap. Of course I came back. That was the plan, wasn't it?"

"To be honest, I have no idea what the plan was, or is, anymore. Can somebody please fill me in on what just happened?"

"We definitely owe you an explanation, Calum," Gabe says. "Ever since you set foot in our agency, things haven't exactly been going according to plan."

"Tell me about it, I still haven't got the foggiest who this Philip Brisbane is."

"That is no coincidence. You got assigned to the wrong family. That's never happened before in the agency's entire existence. At the time I thought it was caused by faulty software. I blamed myself for not being able to get the issue resolved. Then I received news from corporate that I was being demoted, and Olga was taking over. I went down without a fight. That I will always regret, cause all of this would have never happened if I hadn't given in so easily."

"What do you mean?"

"Olga was in league with Seth and Ms Finch from the beginning. The three of them wanted to stir things up at the agency, and take on corporate. Olga meddled with your assignment letter, so you ended up with the Cavendishes, instead of Philip Brisbane. On top of that, she hacked my computer, compromising my software, for which I was blamed, and fired. Once she took over from me as office manager, she kept close tabs on you, Calum. She got wind of your special connection to Randell and wanted to figure out how that happened. Olga assigned me to your parents, knowing I couldn't talk to you about my job. Clever as you are, she counted on you figuring things out by yourself and taking matters into your own hand. Which you did by trying to help out your parents. Then she turned you in, making sure you ended up with this ridiculous re-education programme. All the while they had plans on running tests on you and Randell in hope of a groundbreaking discovery concerning your extraordinary and unique connection.

"They would have taken Randell's life."

"Corporate would have never approved of that, which explains why they kept their little business under the radar."

"But somehow you caught on?"

"Initially, I didn't. Until I got assigned to help out your parents. I told Olga I couldn't take the job, cause I would have to keep you in the dark. She didn't seem to care much. Calum, I felt awful avoiding you like I did. You didn't deserve that."

"My parents didn't deserve to be left on their own like that. When I went down there to see for myself, they were in such a bad place."

"I did try to help them. But I was in over my head. I asked Olga to reassign me multiple times, but she said I was doing just fine. That day you saw me at the Cheeky Rooster with her, I threatened to report her to corporate. She promised to take over from me herself. That hardly made me feel any better, though. I had a hunch she was in on something scathy. On top of that, I had lost my letter of assignment the night you followed me out of the Cheeky Rooster. I figured you found it. A little later, you were arrested in Olga's office. As soon as I heard you were being picked up by a couple of navy blue suits, I knew it was bad. Olga didn't put up much of a fight to keep you with us. From that moment on, I knew for certain she was involved."

"What took you so long to come to my rescue?"

"I had to convince corporate Olga was bad news. Couldn't just walk in there, claiming their recently appointed manager had ulterior motives, and was sabotaging the agency."

"So, what did you do?"

"Well Calum, if you can't beat em, join them. There was a vacancy at corporate, which I applied for. Surprisingly, I got a job as junior adviser. Once I was in, I finally had a chance to voice my concerns to the right people."

"They believed you?"

"Yes and no. They agreed circumstances were suspicious, to say the least, but I had to gather evidence before they were going to take action."

"That's where I came in," Andrew interrupts.

"You certainly did, my dear," Gabe replies.

"What happened after Ms Finch send you on your way to join the agency?"

"I ended up right at Olga's desk. I told her everything I knew, and that we had to take immediate action before it was too late. Olga said she would start making phone calls straight away. She disappeared into her office for a while, but I could still make out what she was saying, more or less. I'm a decent lip reader."

"Sorry, you can read lips?" I ask.

"Back when I was alive, we had quite a substantial number of staff. One of my footmen was mute. His vocal chords suffered severely during a disease he caught in childhood. He could still mouth words to me tough. It took some time getting used to, but after a while, our communication ran rather smoothly. I managed to pick up a word or two from Olga, which wasn't very reassuring. She was talking to Seth, telling him I was kicking up a fuss at the agency."

"So if you didn't get anywhere with Olga, what did you do next?"

"I distinctly remember you telling me about the Cheeky Rooster and how to get there. So that's where I went. At the bar I ran into Mr J-dog."

"It's just J-dog, Andrew. But yes, he ran into me. At first I found his story hard to believe, but then he showed me that exam you took. I know we've only talked a few times, but from the moment I met you, I knew you weren't a liar. That essay of yours shook me to my core, Calum."

"Speaking of which, how did you get it up there, Andrew?"

"During our final exam, I took a little peek at what you were writing, and realised it could be of use. I tried to make eye contact with you, but you wouldn't take the hint. As we were getting ready to leave for the break area, I bumped into our table on purpose. Amidst all your exams flying every which way, I managed to grab your essay."

"Ms Finch did mention one of them was missing."

"After I read your essay exposing Olga, Seth and Ms Finch, I knew I couldn't just stand by and do nothing," J-dog continues.

"So, what did you do?"

"I had a little word with my parent."

"The CEO? I thought you said you hadn't talked to Them in millennia."

"That's what I tell most people. I don't want anyone getting any ideas about me being some kind of shortcut, whenever someone has a grievance. I don't see or speak to Them on a daily basis. This seemed urgent enough, though."

"So what did They say?"

"Not much. They are not very talkative. They did say, they'd be taking care of things, and not to worry. When I got back to the Cheeky Rooster, Gabe was there, staring at Andrew as if he'd seen a ghost."

"Which is technically true. I am dead, after all," Andrew adds helpfully.

"My supervisor at corporate informed me there had been an unexpected breakthrough in the case I was building against Olga. He told me to report to J-dog as soon as possible," Gabe interrupts. "When I arrived at the pub, I couldn't believe my eyes. Andrew was at the bar. I walked up to him, he turned around, and said…"

"Sorry I'm late, my love," Andrew adds, smiling.

"To which I replied, only by a century, darling."

"After our brief reunion, we didn't have time to celebrate. Andrew took the first available elevator down to the Cavendishes to watch over Randell. J-dog and I came down here, hoping we'd find you in one piece."

"So what happens now?" I ask.

"Randell and his family are being watched around the clock by two of our most experienced and trusted agency employees. The same goes for your parents, Calum. I've been asking after their wellbeing constantly. They're doing loads better, ever since you've visited them. They're finally getting the help they need. It was actually quite clever of you to text their closest circle of friends. They rallied around them, making them feel loved and seen."

"What about Olga, Seth and Ms Finch? What's going to happen to them?"

"That's up to corporate. For the time being, it's still undecided."

"Right, one more thing. I was taking this course with several others, all of whom didn't pass. Ms Finch sent them someplace else with just a snap of her fingers. I was wondering if you know where they ended up."

"Ms Finch sent them back to where they all started their afterlife, the waiting room. Corporate is retrieving them as we speak. They'll receive proper counselling and guidance until we've found a suitable destination for them."

"So you don't get sent to a garbage disposal dump if you're deemed unfit to join the agency?"

"Heavens no Calum, there's more to the afterlife than just the agency."

"Didn't get the impression there was."

"You're absolutely right. It was wrong of us to rush down dwellers straight from the waiting room to the agency, without a proper briefing. We've been too focused on getting employees out there in the field as quickly as possible, without realising an extensive introduction wouldn't have gone amiss. We're working on improving that trajectory. Having said that, someone at the agency wants to have a word with you. Can I take you there?"

"Of course, I'm not in trouble, am I?"

"Calum, if anything, you've saved the day."

"Okay. I guess I'll see you in a bit then, J-dog, Andrew?"

"See you later, my man," J-dog says.

"Have a good one, old chap," Andrew adds.

"I'll see you later, my love?" Gabe asks while briefly taking Andrew's hand in his.

"Absolutely Mr Wandsworth. Please don't dawdle. We've got lots to catch up on."

"Duly noted dear."

Gabe and I leave the classroom. I spent the last two days preparing for my reintegration at the agency. Gabe takes my hand, closes his eyes, and says afterlife agency. Within the blink of an eye I'm back in Olga's office. Only it's not her office anymore, nor is it Gabe's.

"Thank you kindly, Mr Wandsworth. I'll take it from here if y'all don't mind."

"Absolutely Mr Presley," Gabe replies. "Calum, I have to go now. Just wanted to say again how sorry I am for everything that's happened. I hope there are no hard feelings between us."

"Of course not Gabe, thanks for saving me, when I thought all hope was lost. You're a good friend. See you in a bit?"

"We'll definitely meet again. Goodbye Calum."

I don't know why this sounded like a final goodbye, but somehow it did. It's been an emotional rollercoaster for all of us, so I'm probably imagining things. Just like the fact that I'm standing right in front of Elvis, who appears to be in charge now.

"Howdy slick, rumour has it the agency has done you dirty."

"Yes, well, uhm, I did get into a spot of bother."

"Sorry to hear that, son. When I heard what they put you through, I was so mad I could chew nails and spit out a barbed wire fence."

"Right, thank you? So I take it you are the new office manager."

"At your service, Sir. Didn't I tell you back at that bar, I wanted to retire from field work?"

"You did. Glad it worked out for you."

"Me too. I'm as happy as if I had good sense. Still, there's lots of work to do to make this a safe place for everyone. First and foremost, for our agency employees."

"So, when do I get back to work?"

"That's what I was hoping to have a word about, son. You see, that gentleman you were originally assigned to didn't make it.

"Philip Brisbane's dead? What happened?"

"No one was assigned to look after Mr Brisbane, after you were sent to the Cavendish family. Gabe was working twenty-four seven figuring out that software glitch, among many other things, and forgot about him. Shortly after he was let go, Olga took over, who turned out to be as worthless as gum on a boot heel. Thing is, everyone was running all over hell's half acre, but no one bothered to think about poor old Philip."

"That's terrible."

"It was. Although Mr Brisbane's situation wasn't dire at first, it did go from bad to worse. He made one poor decision about getting into his car after spending the night drinking at a bar. Add bad weather, and a slippery road to the equation, and there he is, in one of our waiting rooms."

"So, what do you want me to do about it?"

"Thing is, son, you were given a raw deal ever since you came up here. Corporate wants to make amends for that. Also, you forged an extraordinary connection with Randell, because he can see, hear and touch you, something that has never occurred before. Our CEO thinks your story with this young man is far from over. So in other words, They're sending you back."

"Beg your pardon? I'm being sent back? How? As far as I know, my body is buried six feet under. Also, my parents would have a stroke, if I were to show up on their doorstep, like the second coming of well, me."

"You obviously can't go as yourself. Thing is, Philip Brisbane isn't six feet under yet. In fact, he's still at the hospital where he's recently been declared brain dead. There's this small window of time in which you can swap places with him. "

"Hold on, why aren't you sending Philip back?"

"We can't. His soul's too damaged to go anywhere without proper guidance and counselling first. He'd make the same mistakes all over again."

"How am I supposed to live my life as Philip Brisbane? I never met the guy. I don't know anything about him."

"Cellular memory. All of Brisbane's memories and skills are stored in every cell of his body. To make things less confusing, yours will be gone. From the moment we send you back, you'll no longer be Calum Jones."

"How am I supposed to find my way back to Randell?"

"If your connection is as strong as we believe it is, you will. Have faith."

I have a hundred questions, and my mind is in overdrive from what I've just been offered. I have no idea what I'm getting myself into, whether I'll find my way back to him, or if he'll even like me as Philip Brisbane. Besides, the afterlife isn't so bad.

I've made friends, and there's ample entertainment in the Cheeky Rooster. I wouldn't mind staying put here. Yet when I think of Randell, I know I'd swim across an ocean just to see him once more. I'd walk the face of the earth to see him smile, or hear him play jazz tunes again. I'm terrified of what my second chance at life has in store for me, but I've got to take it. For Randell, and for me.

"Alright, I suppose I'll take my chances down there again."

"Nice meeting you, slick, and best of luck with yon fella."

Before I can think of anything else to say, the King of Rock & Roll has snapped his fingers.

Chapter Fourteen

Being back on the soccer pitch feels so good. I haven't been able to play for months, ever since my accident. The doctors said I got lucky. I was basically declared dead, when all of a sudden the heart monitor started beeping again. I don't remember anything of the night I crashed my car. My doctors call it amnesia and think my memory will come back in time. So far it hasn't. Waking up in a hospital bed with more than a few broken bones has been the weirdest sensation ever. I'm not just talking about the psychical pain that comes with having pins stuck in your leg, and casts around both arms. I felt like a completely different person, too. As if I had woken up from a long, restless sleep with very vivid dreams. I can't remember what I dreamt about, though. Perhaps I was reliving the months before I ended up in the hospital. I wasn't doing so great back then. Last year, I dislocated my knee and tore a few ligaments. Despite intense physio therapy my progress was slow. For someone who's made a career out of playing soccer, that really sucks. I was asked to consider other career paths, in case I wasn't going to make a full recovery. Soccer is my life, it always has been. Like any other athlete, I made sacrifices to get this far. After school I went straight to practise, four times a week. I had extra practise on weekends, in addition to games and tournaments. My social life was having a laugh with the other lads in the dressing room after a training session or a match. My dating life was non-existent. I've had the occasional flirt with both boys and girls on a rare night off. But nothing ever lasted. Soccer always came first.

The new me was willing to fight again. At every available opportunity I did the exercises my physio prescribed me. I gritted my teeth when walking felt like torture, and catching so much as a ball was agony. I pulled through, cause deep down inside, for whatever reason, I knew it would all be worth it. Six months after I woke up after intensive surgery, I'm back on the pitch. During my time at the hospital, I had this roomie suffering from ALS. I promised him that as soon as I was back on my feet, I'd organise a charity match to raise money for research. ALS is a disease that causes progressive degeneration to the nerve cells in your spinal cord and brain. It seriously affects control of the muscles you need for important bodily functions, and everyday activities like moving, eating, sleeping, speaking, and even breathing. I can't imagine what it feels like to slowly lose control over the most basic stuff your body is supposed to be capable of. I do know what it's like to be incapacitated due to serious injuries. My discomfort was temporary though, and it didn't get worse, it got better. I'm still a bit stiff in the legs, but I can walk that off. The team we're playing against are relatives, friends, and acquaintances of people suffering from ALS. The atmosphere is amazing. The crowd is cheering everyone on, and although each team is going for the win, there is no animosity between us. After the referee blows his final whistle, we've won by 3-1. Like professional players we swap shirts with our competitors, and shake hands like we've known each other for ages.

One guy has caught my eye from the beginning. He's got strawberry blond hair. His curls are dancing around his angelic face every time he runs for the ball. He frequently pushes them out of his face, but they quickly bounce back the moment he lets go. It's an adorable sight. At one point in the match we accidentally bump into each other. He smiles and asks if I am alright. His almond-shaped brown eyes take my breath away. I nod, cause I can't come up with anything coherent to say. I am not one to take initiative whenever I fancy someone, but somehow I am drawn to him. Right now he's standing ten feet away, drinking from a water bottle. I casually walk up to him.

"Hey, uhm, good match, by the way. You play well."

"Oh hi, thanks. You really think so? I only started training about six months ago."

"Same here. I was in the hospital recovering from an accident. Before I played professionally."

"You looked plenty professional out there to me."

"Ah thanks. So, who are you here for, if you don't mind me asking?"

"My ex-girlfriend's brother has ALS. She asked me to join the team."

"Wow, your ex-girlfriend? Well, you did a really good job today. I'll bet she regrets breaking up with you."

"Who said she broke up with me?"

"Sorry, no one. It's not any of my business either. I'm sorry."

"You're right though, she did break up with me."

"You don't have to tell me, really."

"It's alright, at the time I was struggling with a couple of things. One of them was accepting I'm not into girls, at least not romantically."

"Oh, what was the other one?"

"Coming to terms with my mum dying. She had been in an accident too, but ended up in a coma. She only got worse, so in the end we had to let her go."

"That's terrible. I'm so sorry for your loss."

"Thanks, but I'm doing better now."

"I've been struggling with my orientation, too. It took quite some time before I realised I was both into girls and boys. It felt really lonely at times."

"I totally get what you mean. I was so caught up in my own world, I even made up an imaginary boyfriend. Pathetic, huh?"

"Of course not. Wish I had made one up. I wouldn't have cried myself to sleep for so many nights."

"Thing is, he felt so real to me. I could see him, hear him, and even touch him at one point. Then one day he disappeared. I never saw him again."

"Maybe you didn't need him anymore."

"Not sure about that, embarrassingly enough I still miss him."

"If I had been your imaginary boyfriend, I'd miss you too. Sorry, that was really cringe."

"I thought it was cute."

"Thanks, kind of you to let me off easy."

"No, seriously, that was a really nice thing to say. Are you doing anything later?"

"What, like, you want to hang out?"

"Only if you want to."

"Yes, I'd love to. I mean, uhm, sure I do."

"I'll go change then, and I'll see you in a bit."

"Great! Uhm sorry, but I didn't catch your name."

"It's Randell, my name's Randell Cavendish."

"Nice to meet you Randell, I'm Philip."

Acknowledgements

My dearest Hilde, I want to thank you for your unwavering support throughout my life and in my still fairly recent writing career. With this being my third work, you never miss a chance to tell me how proud you are and how much you believe in me. From the moment we met at the start of our freshman year in college, I knew I had found a soulmate in you—someone I could confide in, share meaningful conversations with, and have uncontrollable giggles over the silliest things. We shared a living space for most of our college years, and having just moved out of my family home with barely the ability to fry an egg, you taught me so much about life and living on my own. I'm so grateful we grew into adulthood together, embracing our newfound independence, stumbling, and getting back up again, all amidst so much love and laughter.

After college, we went our separate ways, yet always found our way back to each other. The great thing about a friendship that goes so far back is celebrating countless milestones together. The past twenty-something years have flown by—it feels like just yesterday we were in our two-bedroom flat, eating mac and cheese four times a week because we were strapped for cash. Years later, even after settling down, we still connect on a level that feels unique to me.

I've always imagined us ending up in a retirement home together—two wrinkly grannies squabbling over a plate of biscuits, causing mischief, and telling endless stories about our children, grandkids, and what everyone's up to. Sadly, life took a different turn. Since I can't imagine a world without you, I've created one—hoping that somehow, we'll always be part of each other's lives, wherever, and in whatever way that may be.

About the Author

My name is Asha Rebel-Lammersen. I was born in India, but grew up in The Netherlands, where I currently live with my diverse, beautiful family.

From an early age I've been fond of reading, and spent hours on end lost in stories and adventures. I started writing when I was about ten years old. I kept journals, wrote short stories, and poems. As I got older, and started adulting I didn't have much free time on my hands. For a while I stopped writing altogether. About a year ago I came up with this story I had wanted to put on paper for a while. I have always been a fan of young, and new adult fiction, especially in the LGTBQ+ genre.

Growing up queer is challenging under the best of circumstances. With nearly two decades of teaching under my belt, I've seen the resilience and pride of many of my queer students, but I've seen their struggles as well. We live in a world where self-determination for women, LGTBQ+, and trans rights are targeted on a daily basis, in countries we would never have thought possible. Harmful pieces of legislation, and homophobic statements from high-ranking members of government are causing immense damage to people who just want to be their true self. I hope my stories will bring joy, comfort, and generally speaking 'a feel-good vibe' to my readers.

Spectrum Books is publishing my second novel, but there are many more to come. Apart from writing I enjoy spending time with family and friends. I work out at the gym regularly to keep somewhat in shape. I like travelling, whenever the opportunity arises. My favourite holiday destinations are Scotland and Ireland. After a hard day's work, I like to unwind in front of the telly with a cup of tea.

Excellent LGBTQ+ fiction by unique, wonderful authors.
Thrillers
Mystery
Romance
Young Adult
& More

Join our mailing list here for news, offers and free books!

Visit our website for more Spectrum Books
www.spectrum-books.com

Or find us on Instagram
@spectrumbookpublisher